Zoe knew

Or maybe sh... everything sh... and touched t... ...ched...ed and touched t... ...smile...she needed to work so hard for what ...d.

And he was the son of the man she'd been hired to shine up in the media, off-limits professionally.

But none of that mattered while his deep green gaze searched her own, as if looking for an answer there—a yes, a no...

Yes, she thought, and she leaned a little closer.

Tyler Barron...

So *not* a good idea.

But that didn't matter.

Then she closed her eyes, waiting to feel him, hoping a hope that had never, ever died since she'd left the ranch.

Dear Reader,

Every family goes through good times and bad. If you're lucky, you have a group who backs you up, and you do the same for them. But there are some times that are trying for even the tightest of families, and this is when you—and they—can really be put to the test.

That's just what happens to the Barrons in the Billionaire Cowboys, Inc. miniseries. There's a family secret that explodes, and it's going to affect each Barron brother dramatically....

I hope you enjoy this first book, which focuses on the eldest brother, Tyler, and how the right woman at the right time helps him to pull through—and how he attempts to mend his family, as well. I also hope you'll join me at www.crystal-green.com, where I've got contests, a blog and updated news.

All the best,

Crystal Green

MADE FOR
A TEXAS
MARRIAGE

CRYSTAL GREEN

SPECIAL EDITION

Published by Silhouette Books

America's Publisher of Contemporary Romance

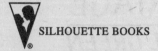

SILHOUETTE BOOKS

ISBN-13: 978-0-373-65575-5

Recycling programs
for this product may
not exist in your area.

MADE FOR A TEXAS MARRIAGE

Copyright © 2011 by Chris Marie Green

Visit Silhouette Books at www.eHarlequin.com

Printed in U.S.A.

Books by Crystal Green

CRYSTAL GREEN

lives near Las Vegas, where she writes for Silhouette Special Edition and Harlequin Blaze. She loves to read, overanalyze movies and TV programs, practice yoga and travel when she can. You can read more about her at www.crystal-green.com, where she has a blog and contests. Also, you can follow her on Facebook at www.facebook.com/people/Chris-Marie-Green/1051327765 and Twitter at www.twitter.com/ChrisMarieGreen.

To Gary—strength and happiness.

Prologue

The night Tyler Barron's world fell apart, he was actually standing at the very top of it.

At least, that was what he felt like as he poured some single-barrel bourbon into his crystal glass then raised it in a toast to his younger brother, Jeremiah.

"Here's to the reason Dad no doubt called us back to the ranch tonight. May his well-earned retirement from The Barron Group allow him plenty of R & R."

Jeremiah lifted his own glass. "And here's to the great Eli Barron finally announcing that he's handing over the reins to his co-vice presidents."

"To the brothers Barron, then."

They clinked glasses, drained their cocktails. But then Jeremiah paused as Tyler prepared another round.

"You really think it'll just be the two of us he'll give control to?" he asked.

"Are you talking about Chet?" Tyler laughed. "Just because he managed a few splashy development deals lately doesn't mean Dad's ready to take a big step like making him a third owner. He's just our cousin, Jer."

"He was invited over tonight, too."

"That's because Chet will probably replace Uncle Abe as CFO. No doubt that's what they're telling him in the study right now."

"I don't know. Dad's taken quite a shine to him."

"Oh, come on—not *that* big a shine."

As Jeremiah shrugged, then drank some more, Tyler's words hovered in his chest, as if staying behind, unwilling to be dismissed.

But he pushed the niggle aside anyway, sitting in a cushiony leather wingchair. Around him, the Barron mansion's lounge gleamed with velvet upholstery and dark woods. An oil painting hung above the fireplace mantel, showing off the proud faces of Eli Barron, his lean, stately late wife, Florence, and their two sons: Tyler with the dark hair and green eyes he'd inherited from Mom, and Jeremiah with the wheat-blond and blue-eyed dash of their father.

In that picture, Tyler stood near his dad, but there was a distance between them. *Art imitating life,* Tyler thought wryly.

He glanced toward the door, where Eli would no doubt arrive soon, probably even with Chet in tow. Dad always seemed to have their cousin near, with his hand on his shoulder, whether it was for an encouraging pat or an affectionate uncle's squeeze.

But why was that such an odd thing when Tyler worked just as closely with Uncle Abe on The Barron Group's media outlets and property holdings and thought of *him* as a father most of the time?

Jeremiah noticed the direction of Tyler's focus. "Dad'll make a grand entrance, as usual—three sheets to the wind."

"Just so he doesn't tax Uncle Abe tonight with his celebrating."

"Abe's nurse is probably in there with them, ready to chase everyone out."

"Abe was on firm ground when he got here earlier. It's been a good day for him." Chemo usually made his uncle's days *less* than good. So did having a son come around after years of estrangement.

At the mention of their ailing uncle, silence hung between the brothers. Things had been different after Chet had been summoned down here from his Montana cattle ranch. His dad was dying, and Eli Barron had given Chet a position in The Barron Group, ostensibly as an incentive to stay alongside his father while they made amends. But Tyler doubted that Chet had needed the pot sweetened in such a way. A decent man stuck by his family through thick and thin.

A door banged open down the hallway, and the brothers glanced at each other.

When boot steps pounded on the floor, Tyler got up to see what was going on.

Chet was walking toward him stiffly, but there was something about his gaze...as if he didn't see Tyler at all. Obviously, he'd taken the news about Tyler and Jeremiah's promotions hard.

"Everything all right?" Tyler asked.

Chet halted for a beat. He looked more like Jeremiah, with that dark blond coloring. But unlike his lean cousin, Chet was a couple inches shorter and hardier. Though he'd been wearing suits since he'd started with The Group, he still looked as if he'd prefer denim and dust-bitten boots.

Once upon a time, Tyler had preferred the ranching life, too, but then he'd embarked upon his rise in The Barron Group. That was his life now—success, designer suits...

He gripped his drinking glass.

Chet started to say something, but when Eli's voice sounded in the background, his skin grew ruddier than Tyler had ever seen it, and he made his way out of the mansion, slamming the front door behind him.

What the hell?

He thought about going after him until Eli stepped out of the study down the hall, saw Tyler, then glanced behind him into the room. Abe was probably still in there.

It was almost as if Abe said something to Eli because, with a deep breath, he put on a smile and came down the hallway.

"I see you two started early." He indicated his son's drink then walked right past him into the lounge, making his way over to the minibar where Jeremiah still waited, just as lethargically as he did almost everything else.

"What's wrong with Chet?" Tyler asked.

"Nothing." Eli Barron waved the question away, picking up a bourbon glass. But he didn't fill it with anything. His flushed complexion spoke to his having imbibed a nip or two in the study.

Tyler coolly raised a brow and took his seat again,

reclining, ankle crossed over his knee, showing a hand-tooled leather boot under the designer suit.

Jeremiah took a spot on a settee. "You going to keep us in suspense all night, Dad?"

The older man exhaled, and when he set down his glass, Tyler noticed that his father's hand was trembling.

"The thing is," Eli said, "I have a lot of personal business to catch you boys up on. I should've done it earlier…" He fumbled with his next words. "The time never did seem right though. But recent events have made explanations necessary—Abe getting sick and deciding to retire along with me, Chet moving down here, then getting settled in The Group." He nodded, as if to himself. "The personal business can't wait any longer."

Then their dad sent a look of cryptic emotion toward the entrance, as if he was expecting—or hoping—Chet would come back in.

Something was happening, and it wasn't necessarily about retirement and promotions.

Jeremiah glanced at Tyler, and he knew his brother felt it, too.

"Dad, why don't you just come out with it?" Tyler said, attacking the suspense head-on.

Eli held up a hand, cutting him off. It was like a slap, and Tyler's temper flared ever so slightly.

"I brought you all here tonight," his dad finally said, "because I decided I'm retiring from The Group and, as you might've guessed, control's going to you both. But it's going to Chet, too."

Tyler's stomach started to sink. Maybe it was in the way his dad's voice seemed a little choked.

Or maybe it was because his father had braced himself on the minibar—which didn't bode well.

If Eli Barron had seemed emotional before, he was doubly so now, his voice strangled. "*All* of my sons have a right to the company I built from the ground up."

Every one of his...

Sons?

The word echoed in Tyler's brain, chiseling something away inside him.

Sons.

Everything Tyler thought he'd ever known seemed to crumble out from under him, toppling him from that top-of-the-world spot he'd been in just minutes ago.

Chapter One

One Week Later

"This is going to be perfect!" said Zoe Velez as she aimed her handheld camera around the field where the county fair was in full swing.

Smoke from the barbecue competition filtered over the patriotic bunting and banners, as well as the strolling locals and tourists in summer clothes who'd come to the village of Duarte Hill to hear country music, eat homemade chili and brave the midway rides. For just one week every year, this small town burst into color and energy that rivaled nearby San Antonio before going quiet again.

As Zoe swept the camera to the right, following the crowds that headed toward the looming Ferris wheel, she remembered her own childhood days at the fair, although she hadn't stuck around after she'd left Florence Ranch all those years ago.

A female voice sounded from next to her. "Ma'am, Jeremiah Barron's meeting us at the ranch in an hour for that interview. Shouldn't we be preparing...?"

Ma'am. Zoe lowered the camera and grinned politely at Ginnifer, the local college student who'd been accepted as an intern with the Walker & Associates PR firm for the summer.

The redhead adjusted her wire-rimmed glasses, as if rethinking her prodding, as well as the appropriateness of calling her thirty-four-year-old boss "ma'am."

Yup, Ginnifer belonged to Zoe, starting today. The administrative staff had assigned the girl at the last minute, and they'd met in the dirt parking lot just about five minutes ago. Ginnifer had no idea how to approach business with Zoe just yet.

But getting an intern was very good news. To the bosses' way of thinking, this assignment deserved the support.

She, Zoe Velez, had finally rated an intern. *Yes!*

Letting the girl's "ma'am" slide, Zoe motioned to a spot where they wouldn't be overheard. "Not to worry, we'll make it to Jeremiah with time to spare. I just want some establishing shots of Duarte Hill in its full glory. When the real film crew comes out here in a few days, the fair's going to be over, and some footage would be handy, just in case they want to use it for local color. It would add a certain down-home quality to the Barron image."

"Right, Ms. Velez." Ginnifer was nodding, taking everything down on her eager-beaver mental notepad while she clutched their carryalls.

Zoe kept her voice low as she filmed their surroundings, watching the footage on the digital camera screen. "Apple pie and family values—everything we want to paint the Barrons with is right here. And they're going to need every bit of positive imagery they can get when this scandal finally hits the media. They've got business holdings all over the world, but their biggest base is in the South, where people won't look kindly upon a man sleeping with his brother's wife and hiding the affair for years."

"I can't believe you've kept it from the press for this long."

"The family's pretty secretive, so they've managed to lie low for the time being. But they know the bomb's going to drop, and they figured it might as well be a controlled explosion. That's why we're in Duarte Hill."

To figure out a plan for the big reveal to the media. To ease into the scandal *Zoe's* way.

"Cool," Ginnifer said, smiling, as if the intern had already figured out what a big break this could be for Zoe's career—and maybe even her own someday. "From the little I heard during my briefing about what Eli Barron did, he'll need a good paintbrush. What a jerk."

Zoe's chin lifted a little. Her intern had no idea just how much of a jerk. But Zoe would deal with Eli Barron—and the rest of his brood—for the sake of this job.

"Ginnifer," she said, as if having to persuade herself, too, "just remember PR 101—no judging the clients."

"Yes, you're right. You're totally right."

Zoe hated to lecture, especially when she, herself, occasionally had doubts about the clients she was hired to paint over sometimes. But she told herself that her job did help people—it softened the reactions of the public for the innocent ones who were caught up in difficult situations. She just tried not to think about what it did for the guilty.

As she and Ginnifer moved on, they passed a charity tent filled with handcrafted auction items like quilts and leatherwork.

"Ma'am?"

"PR 101, rule number two—no calling me 'ma'am' or 'Ms. Velez.' I'm Zoe, okay?"

"Yes, ma—Zoe." The intern gripped her bags tighter as one strap began to fall from her shoulder. "You already know the Barrons, right? And that's why Mr. Walker assigned you to this?"

Zoe's pride stood on end and, again, she made sure no one was around to listen. "My father was a foreman at Florence Ranch until recently, so, yes, I did spend a few years there. But I had to lobby for this assignment." She shrugged. "It probably didn't hurt that I kicked some major butt on the Lira political campaign."

She wasn't going to add how she'd left the ranch—ten years old and feeling as if she had her tail between her legs. She wasn't going to think about bygones at all. Wasn't going to think about how the kids at school had called her "servant" or how the arrogant Barrons had made her father feel like a lesser man.

She wasn't even going to think about how she used to stare up at that big mansion, dreaming about a day when she, too, could live like they did *and* without all the advantages that'd gotten them there....

Ginnifer seemed happy with Zoe's answers. "Did you know the Barron brothers? They're cute."

For heaven's sake. "I knew them a little. When we

were really young, Tyler and Jeremiah used to sneak out of the big house to play with us ranch rats when they were home from boarding school. Their parents would have a cow every time they found out about it. It's not like I really *knew* them, though."

Sneaking out to play hadn't meant Tyler or Jeremiah had been just like the other kids on the ranch. Tyler, especially, had been bossy. And while he hadn't seemed as blatantly superior as his father, Zoe had assumed that he would get to that point eventually. After all, he was a Barron.

Zoe's mind wandered to those days of playing hide-and-seek in the old barn. In spite of her misgivings about Tyler, she'd always found herself hoping that the golden boy with the sunshine crowning his dark hair would find her.

He never had.

Then had come the darker times after the whole situation with Eli Barron—how he'd mistreated her dad with just a couple of ill-conceived words after the boss had found some fences knocked down. Broken fences that her father had just discovered.

Lazy Mexican.

Things hadn't been the same after that. Her mom had kept her away from the Barron boys. Then, finally, away from the ranch altogether after Eli Barron had degraded her father and her mother had lost respect for him, divorcing him.

Zoe adjusted the camera. "What I'm trying to say is Tyler probably won't even remember me, if and when he decides to return my phone calls. Jeremiah barely recalled me when I asked to make an appointment for an interview with him. Chet didn't grow up on the ranch, so I didn't know him in the first place."

Ginnifer looked as if she was going to ask more questions, but Zoe took off, walking toward the midway.

There, she got some establishing footage before they went back to the exhibit lanes. The intern dutifully followed, just as Zoe had done during her own trip up the career ladder, scrapping her way from a poor ranch rat to the here and now.

They were passing a stage where an old cowboy was reciting some range poetry, and she ran the camera lens over the crowd, then continued toward the outskirts, to the fringes where a lone man was leaning against a power pole.

She fixed the lens on his weathered boots, then panned up faded jeans that encased long, muscled legs. Slim hips, lean waist, flat stomach, a pair of strong arms crossed over a wide chest covered by a light blue Western shirt. And his shoulders...

They were broad, too, but for some reason, Zoe got the impression that a lot seemed to be weighing on them.

When she got to his face, her heart jerked, fisting and unfisting as if trying to grasp something she'd lost over the years. Or maybe it was something she'd never had at all.

Tyler Barron.

His face, with its firm, dimpled chin, was shaded by his cowboy hat, but she knew his eyes would be a deep green, his hair a rich chocolate-brown.

She hadn't seen Tyler in a long time—especially not this way. In all the photos she'd reviewed, he'd looked like a winner-take-all billionaire in designer suits, attending charity functions and political events.

But this Tyler?

He was the guy who used to ride the ranch, so natural in the saddle. Yet, somewhere along the line, he'd fully become the Tyler who'd been chauffeured up the driveway to and from boarding school during vacation time. The boy groomed by his father to rule the business world. Even back then, when she was only ten—the same age as Tyler—it was obvious that he'd been destined to be more than a cowboy.

And that he and Zoe would never live in the same world again.

But now that space between them filled up with a long exhalation from Zoe, who was all grown up and closer than ever to being in the Barrons' stratosphere. In fact, she held the cards for their family.

She wasn't a ranch rat anymore.

Realizing that she had a job to do, she shut off the camera.

She'd heard that Tyler was taking a sabbatical from The Barron Group in the aftermath of Eli's announcement, probably because of the family scandal. But it just seemed odd that a nonstop businessman like him was out here, enjoying a country fair, rather than working side by side with Jeremiah in the city right now.

It was Zoe's job to find out why he was here instead, in cowboy clothes, standing apart from everyone.

She took another deep breath, heat creeping through her body, warming her belly as if it were filled with milk, simmering and threatening to melt her.

Then a pop of resentment flared in her, but this time, the heat had nothing to do with attraction.

Was she *really* going to stand here and act like a girl who wasn't as good as the rich family?

"Zoe?" Ginnifer asked.

Great. Here she was, having a hot flash in the middle of the fair. Even her intern had noticed.

Zoe relieved Ginnifer of one of the carryalls, slinging it over her shoulder, where it crumpled her otherwise professional white linen sleeveless blouse. She handed the camera over to her intern.

"Catch some more of that local color, okay? We'll meet back here in fifteen."

For some reason, she didn't want Ginnifer there when she approached Tyler. Maybe she was afraid she would be blushing too much, even though her skin tone hid that pretty well. Still, rising PR stars didn't blush.

"Gotcha," Ginnifer said, happily taking the camera and wandering toward a tent in which a cowboy was cracking a whip from the safety of a stage, exhibiting his prowess.

Zoe smoothed down her shirt as best as she could, her heart beating beneath it so hard that she could've sworn the linen fluttered. She tucked a strand of straight-edged, neck-length hair behind her ear, then exhaled, realizing she'd just been holding her breath.

Caramba.

She glanced at Tyler again and frowned. *The lone cowboy.* Where was the self-assured Barron scion she remembered?

Raising her chin, she moved toward him, but the closer she came, the more her heart took over, stamping through her veins, tattooing her skin from the inside out. Things even looked a little surreal as her head went light.

She stood next to him, but it took him a moment to realize that someone was there. Even in that short time, she caught the scent of him—leather and soap.

Like old times on the ranch.

When he did look at her, something clicked in his green gaze. But it couldn't have been recognition: it had been so long since she'd seen him and, even then, they hadn't really known each other.

Then a smile crept over his mouth, and Zoe felt as if she was the only woman in the world.

Yet as soon as it was there, it was gone, leaving Zoe to try to breathe again like a normal person, fighting off a blush that was powerful enough to make even *her* skin blaze like a five-alarm fire.

The Barron arrogance. He had it, all right. And it had probably even reached Eli Barron proportions by now.

"Tyler?" she asked, all business.

One of his eyebrows cocked slightly, but that hint of a smile never came back. It was as if he remembered he was supposed to be the boss of everything, including her.

She took the initiative and offered a hand for a shake. "You probably don't remember me, but I'm Zoe Velez. Miguel the old foreman's daughter."

It was obvious when he recalled her, maybe because he was vaguely remembering one of the many ranch rats who'd splashed in the swimming hole.

Or was he thinking about the girl who'd left with her mom, abandoning her dad, never to return?

No, he wouldn't focus on that. She hadn't been important enough to him.

Not in the way she was about to be.

"Zoe?" he said in a deep voice that she felt all the way down to her toes, even though he'd lent a civil distance to her name.

And, just like that, she started to melt again.

When Tyler had first seen her, he'd recognized her.

But it wasn't in a way that allowed him to recall her name, or exactly *who* she was. She'd only seemed familiar enough to send a twang of…something…through him that deserted him even before he could identify it.

All he knew was that, whatever it was about her, it felt comfortable. Real. Unlike everything else he'd been through lately.

Then she'd told him her name, and he'd barely thought of a little girl—a ranch kid who'd been just as much of a country miss as he'd been a cowboy. It had reminded him of who he used to be before they'd *all* changed.

As he perused her, his heart clenched again, just as it had when he'd first laid eyes on her—when he hadn't even recognized the old foreman's daughter and he'd only been reacting to a gorgeous woman coming toward him. Even now, an afterburn trailed through Tyler, sizzling in places he preferred to keep cold.

Cold was good right now. It allowed him to recover. Allowed him to take a more aloof look at everything around him.

Even Zoe Velez.

Her straight, dark brown hair was cut short, in a style that came to her neck and slightly flipped up at the ends. She'd lost any and all baby fat, easing the transition from blue jeans and flower-eyelet tops to a pair of khaki trousers and a no-nonsense blouse that showed off toned arms. The dusky skin she'd inherited from her half-Mexican father brought out her white mother's blue-gray eyes, making Zoe seem…exotic, almost delicate.

She was standing there, obviously waiting for him to utter something else besides her name.

Buried anger—at his family, at the world—forced him to prove that he was in control of the situation. Being in control was the only thing he did have control of right now.

"Are you visiting Duarte Hill?" he finally asked.

"Yes. It's been a while though." Her voice was sweet, soothing and mellow. "My mom took me to the city when my parents split up, and my dad would visit me there."

Divorce? He'd gone through his own a few years ago, and now he felt as if it was happening again with his very own family.

Then she threw a curveball into the conversation. "Are you on vacation back at the ranch?"

"Pretty much."

She didn't need to know about how, after his dad's shocking announcement, Tyler had gotten over the numbness all too quickly and blown up. How Eli Barron had told Tyler to cool off and take some time to get his act together. How it had shamed Tyler to be so easily cast aside when all he'd done his whole life was devote himself to the Barrons.

Jeremiah had seemed equally angry at Eli, too, but they'd had different ways of coping. His brother had shut down, hiding behind an uncaring facade, as always. In the past, Tyler had always suspected that Jer had felt like the "disposable son," although he'd rather die than show any dents in his confidence. He'd actually flaunted a playboy image, as if to prove to their father that being disposable had its freedoms, and he was all for enjoying them.

But now Jeremiah had all but submerged himself in an endless round of parties and women, although he was still an ace at work. Yet behind the mask, Tyler knew better.

As for Chet, Tyler had heard through his administrative assistant that even *he* had drawn into himself, going to the site of a spa development project he was overseeing in Utah.

Surprisingly, Eli hadn't chased after his "new" son. He'd taken off to New York, seeing to some supposedly urgent business he needed to deal with before officially retiring. And maybe it was best that he wasn't around, since that allowed Tyler to make arrangements to keep Abe in the mansion rather than in his house near the city. Tyler, himself, had taken up temporary residence in a staff cabin, where he could stay near Abe while not having to be in the mansion, should his father come home unexpectedly.

Abe was the real victim here. Good God, while he was undergoing *chemo* his own brother had made this announcement to the family. But Abe had handled the scandal with a great deal of grace, saying that the truth had to come out sometime.

That was when his nurse had put his foot down and insisted on some rest, and Tyler hadn't pursued the matter with Abe since then, thinking his uncle didn't need the drama.

Now, Zoe's voice soothed into him. "What big plans do you have during your vacation?"

This talk was easy enough, so Tyler answered. "It's been a long time since I was on the ranch, so I'm taking advantage of it while I can. Riding, working the land, watching the sunsets from my porch..." He was surprised at how wistful he sounded.

The ranch—not the mansion—was a place that brought back the days when life hadn't seemed so complicated.

"Well, it seems your time off is agreeing with you," she said.

"I'm also there because my uncle's sick and he needs support. I don't know if you heard about his cancer."

"I did, and I'm really sorry, Tyler."

She glanced away from him, almost as if...

As if she knew more than even that.

She bit her lip, as if she was mulling something over. His gaze lingered on her mouth, which was full, a deep pink, and he was sure the color wasn't from any lipstick. He wanted to run his thumb over it, just to be sure, but he dismissed the notion.

Too bad his body didn't do the same, because it was throbbing, reminding him of how long it'd been since he'd needed a woman. There'd been dates after his divorce—mostly business get-togethers—but he hadn't *needed* for a long time. He'd forced himself to ignore those feelings out of pure survival instinct after Kristen. Then he'd seemed to need work more than play.

Zoe saw him staring at her mouth, and she pursed her lips, as if banishing the temptation.

He straightened up from his spot against the pole. Nearby, the crowd applauded at the end of the old cowboy's poetry reading, then began to wander off to other amusements.

She waited until they were nearly alone, then said, "I've also heard about...other situations in your family."

He froze as the words sank in. Had she said what he thought she'd just said?

How did she know when they'd kept it so quiet?

Then it dawned on him, and his temper spiked. "Your dad must've mentioned it."

"No, it wasn't my dad—"

She was about to add more, but Tyler was already saying, "I guess that PR firm The Group hired for damage control better step on it, huh? I wish the scandal wranglers the best of luck shining up the wreckage."

At his sharp tone, her eyes got a bit wider, but his temper was still doing the talking for him.

"Anyone who even tries to make Eli Barron come out of this as a good guy is just as low-down as *he* is in my book."

She lowered her gaze, then slowly brought it back up to him. "You *want* your dad to look bad?"

It was an innocent question, but it was testing the bounds of small talk with a person he was barely acquainted with.

Who was Zoe Velez to even ask about this? How could she, a virtual stranger, even *know* how everything had affected him? Or how much he had sacrificed for The Barron Group, his family...all for something that had turned out to be a lie?

The anger burned even stronger in him. Thanks to this forced sabbatical, he'd been able to tuck emotion away after the first explosion of temper with his father. But now that the subject was out there, he was livid not just for Uncle Abe, but...

He thought of that portrait with his mom in it, unsmiling, so serious under her teased brown hair.

When she'd died seven years ago in a car accident with Aunt Laura, had she known about all this? Had she been dreading the day her husband would reveal the truth, or had she been blissfully unaware?

"As far as my father goes," Tyler said, closing out this damn discussion, "he made his bed. Now everyone else has to lie down in it, and he's not affected in the least. He left us all to simmer, and he thinks that some PR is going to turn down the heat."

"You don't think a little help would—"

"Help?" He throttled that anger. "Thanks to Eli Barron, this family has been torn into a million pieces. Nothing's going to *help* that, and anyone who tries to spin it differently isn't going to find it easy."

He noticed a change in Zoe—a lifting of her chin, a fire in her eyes.

"You'd stand in the way of whoever your dad hired to help The Barron Group?" she asked.

"Instead of excusing him from everything, including being here, facing the consequences, apologizing his ass off to his own brother—instead of escaping on a business trip? You bet. I guess I'd be pretty uncooperative in that respect."

"Tyler," she said on a sigh, and he knew he was about to hear something he didn't want to. "Just so you know," she added, "I didn't hear a word of your family situation from my dad. I heard it in my office."

Tyler shut down, almost enough so that her next words barely made it through to him.

"*I'm* the scumbag your company hired to clean up your family scandal."

Chapter Two

That same day, after Jeremiah left for his condo penthouse in the city after their interview, Zoe stayed at the family estate, the ranch that had been named after the late Mrs. Eli Barron.

Florence.

Jeremiah had been the one who'd suggested that Zoe stay in one of the guesthouses near the mansion, and she'd settled into the little Swiss-looking cottage with purple, white and yellow perennials spilling out of window boxes. In spite of Jeremiah's reputation for enjoying the company of women—especially after the scandal had broken—Zoe hadn't detected anything but a professional concern for her convenience when he'd extended this invitation to temporarily reside on the property. An ex-ranch rat was possibly even beneath the seduction efforts of the notoriously flirtatious brother, and she didn't exactly have the social pedigree a Barron would be drawn to.

From her cottage window, she could look out at the big house, which was what they used to call it. Probably still did, too. Nowadays, though, it didn't seem as big or daunting to her, just as Jeremiah hadn't, either. But when she and Ginnifer had taken iced tea on the patio by the pool to talk with the second eldest Barron brother, she hadn't been able to keep her eyes off the Greek Revival stateliness of the mansion, the promises that had driven her for years.

After dismissing Ginnifer for the day, Zoe had gone down to her dad's cabin, which was a far cry from the mansion—or even Zoe's guesthouse—in appearance. The pine porch and rugged exterior spoke of Texas simplicity. So did the hunting gear and faux-cowhide upholstery on the inside.

Still, to Zoe, the cabin was somewhat of a prize, but only because her father had earned it after his years of loyal service to the Barrons, who'd given it to him as a retirement gift.

After closing the door behind her, Zoe found her dad sleeping on the sofa, his breath sawing in and out. He'd been breathing that way ever since a bout with pneumonia a little over a month ago. She'd jumped at the chance to stay in the guesthouse partly so she could see how he was doing as well as the convenience of being on the property with the Barrons; this way, she didn't have to drive back and forth from her apartment in San Antonio.

Also, there was the little matter of closure with her dad. Forgiveness for what had happened with their family.

Bending to the couch, she kissed him on a withered cheek, then stood to really look at him.

No one told us about this part of growing up.

She had her dad, and Tyler had Uncle Abe, both of whom needed extra care now from the younger generation.

Tyler.

Heaviness stole over her at the memory of him to-day—the disappointment in his eyes when she'd told him that she was the one who'd be working on "shining up" the scandal.

But she shrugged off the feeling and went to the kitchen, unloading the cloth shopping bags she'd filled with vegetables, tortillas and other goodies for making burritos. Even though she was quiet, her dad stirred awake, then came into the kitchen, hugging her and taking a sprawling seat in a chair at the oak table.

"You're full of steam today." When he was tired, his voice adopted more of an accent than usual.

"I'm just making dinner."

"And you're doing it angrily. I knew it would happen after you started this job for the Barrons."

Why did her dad have to be so eagle-eyed?

She turned to find him watching her, with a slight slant to his brow. He had wrinkles around his mouth and leathery, tanned skin from years of working outside, although he also seemed more drawn these days. His wavy salt-and-pepper hair was mussed from his nap, as were his T-shirt and jeans.

She tried not to think that he was someone to be pitied, as her mother thought everyone pitied them after The Situation—the day of Eli Barron's "lazy Mexican" slur.

"I talked with Jeremiah," she said, "just to get his take on the issues. It seems as if he's taking the scandal in stride on the surface, but from what I recall of him, he was good at acting as if nothing much bothered him at all. I'll be talking to Chet on the phone tomorrow."

"And Tyler?"

Ding-ding-ding. Her dad had nailed the source of her steam.

But she didn't want to talk about Tyler. Unlike Jeremiah, he seemed to have taken the PR cleanup personally, as if she'd been hired to erase Eli Barron's sins, not make them palatable to a world that did business with their media outlets and property holdings.

Tyler thought she was dirt for even being a part of this.

The area around her heart stung, probably because she'd wondered if choosing to shine up Eli Barron was the right thing to do, too, especially with what he'd done to her dad.

But maybe the sting mostly came from being the young girl who'd had a bit of a crush on Tyler. And maybe that girl had thought a grown-up Tyler would see her as the woman she'd worked so hard to become—a woman who was just here to help him and his family.

"I saw him at the fair," Zoe said. "We only had a brief conversation, but he made it cuttingly clear that my PR endeavors weren't welcome."

"Well, *mija,* forgive me for saying so, but Tyler's always had a strong sense of justice. That's why he's such a leader."

"He's a leader because he was born with all the advantages of one, just like any other Barron."

"Now that's your mom talking, isn't it? She would've lumped them together like that."

Zoe pursed her lips. She didn't want to sound like Mom, because she'd spent a lot of time listening to her bitterness, the reminder of why there had been a divorce in the first place—because of those Barrons. Zoe hadn't even told her mother that she'd taken this job yet, probably because she didn't want to deal with the reaction.

She grabbed an emptied bag, folding it. "I keep telling myself that it isn't my job to judge people like the Barrons. It's to bring out the best in them, even if they've done something wrong. And that's what I'll do during this project—I swear I will."

"If Eli Barron regretted his indiscretions, it would certainly make it all the easier." A hint of emotional pain crept into his tone.

Zoe didn't point it out, but she knew he was thinking about his own divorce from her mom. Sure, it'd been amicable—he'd agreed to visitation instead of a custody fight, thinking Zoe was better off in the city, where she would fulfill her high ambitions, even the ones she'd nursed at a tender age. But being left by the woman you loved couldn't ever be easy, especially if she'd come to resent you for not standing up for yourself against your boss when he got frustrated and said something ugly….

Zoe put aside the reminder of how the Barrons treated people, even though she'd wondered if she could wash away everything about the family with some good PR.

Putting down the shopping bag, she said, "You know how much this assignment means to me."

"Yes, I do. And I know that you just want to be recognized for all your efforts...by everyone."

"You say that as if I have some kind of chip on my
shoulder and I'm daring the Barrons to knock it off."

"Isn't that the case?"

Once again, she heard echoes in her mind of the kids
at school calling out, "Servant girl! Servant girl!"

Grabbing a couple of green and red bell peppers,
she went to the sink to clean them, then put the subject
firmly back where she wanted it.

"Talking about chips on the shoulder, I see that Tyler
is taking some time away from work right now."

"Is this where you press me for details about the
family, now that you've landed this assignment?"

"I use every resource I can." But she wouldn't stress
her dad out about this. If there was too much strain in
his voice, she'd stop. "From what I hear, Tyler hasn't
taken many vacations in his life."

Behind Zoe, her dad sighed, as if resigned to his
fate as her mole. "Gossip from the big house has it that,
after Eli told them his news, Tyler ripped into his father.
Of course, a man with Eli's ego wasn't having any of
it, so he told Tyler that he needed to take time off and
gain some perspective—and if he couldn't get his act
together again, he wouldn't be welcome back into The
Group."

Zoe frowned. She hadn't known that part, either. No
wonder Tyler seemed so distant and bottled up with
fury. She would be ready to explode, too.

"Did Chet take off to Utah because he needed a
break, too?" she asked.

"Yes, but it wasn't one that Eli imposed on him.
And I imagine Chet will be back soon now that Eli's

away. He's tried to be a good son after all the years
of estrangement between him and Abe, so I can't see
him being gone for too long. A number of months ago,
when he heard about his dad's—well, the man who he
thought was his dad's—cancer, he sold his cattle business and came right on down to work for The Barron
Group, but that's only because Abe was always after
Chet to become more than a rancher. Chet had rebelled
before, but with the sickness, he gave in to his father's
wishes."

"Tyler had to bristle a little at that, don't you think?
He was always meant to be the number one son."

"He knew a reconciliation was best for the family
as a whole, so he accepted Chet's fast-tracking in the
company. But Tyler was never one to wear his emotions
on his sleeve—just like Jeremiah. Not until Eli forced
him to burst."

Zoe started drying the vegetables, using woven cloth
towels with sharp pinwheel designs sewn into them,
almost like little explosions themselves. "You know how
Tyler seemed to me today? Like a stranger, Poppy. A
stranger in his own hometown."

Her dad leaned forward, propping his arms on
the table. "I'd feel the same way, with what he's gone
through these past few years. His mom's death. Abe's
sickness. This scandal... Sometimes I think that he even
loves his uncle more than he does his own father and
this cancer has hit him deep and hard. They worked
together just about hand in hand at The Group, you
know. Eli and Tyler didn't ever seem as close, and now
that Eli has shown his true colors, I suppose Tyler's
affection for his uncle has grown even stronger."

"Maybe staying here on the property with Abe, even

during a sabbatical from his job, is Tyler's way of showing his dad where his allegiance lies. It's a statement. So is the fact that he's living in a worker cabin, as if *he's* rebelling against everything his dad ever wanted from him."

"I'll bet you're right on that. But Tyler's intentions are good. He wants to make sure his uncle's comfortable, too."

She knew what it was like to have a loved one fall sick. Her dad didn't have cancer, but when she'd gotten a call from Keith, the new foreman, saying he was taking her father to the hospital, it had been as if someone had yanked the ground out from under her.

Her dad tapped the table with his fingertips. "But even before all that, Tyler had his ex-wife to contend with."

A trickle of curiosity ran through her. "I heard about the divorce in passing from you, but I don't know the details. The Barrons used a different PR firm a few years ago."

"All I really know was that Tyler was fortunate to be rid of that woman, even if Eli wasn't happy about it. He highly approved of Kristen. I wouldn't be surprised if, way in the back of Tyler's mind, he talked himself into marrying her because she was perfect in his father's eyes." Miguel stopped for a second, then said, "Tyler's always been that family man, and I suspect he looks at Eli's betrayal as a slap in the face to everything that he's ever invested in the Barrons and their business."

Zoe understood. Family was everything, and in retrospect, she would've gone the extra mile to hold her own together, too.

People who wanted to be the best sons and daughters did that. But at what cost?

Maybe such a sacrifice would've made her just as resentful as Tyler was if it'd been thrown right back in her face. And hadn't she even felt a bit of that after her own parents had divorced? Her situation didn't come anywhere near the Barrons' in terms of spectacular ruins, but that single separation had hurt her just the same, even to the point where she didn't trust many people, either.

To the point where, like Tyler, she worked and worked, shunting aside her personal life, unless you counted things like online dating sites and the infrequent dates she went on as a result.

"Anyway," Miguel continued, "after the divorce, Tyler labored like a dog, and he did so until this sabbatical forced him out."

Letting up on the questioning with her dad, Zoe cut the peppers. He didn't know it, but she was serving a meat-free meal. She was fooling him with soy "beef" tonight because his dietary habits had raised a flag for his doctor, and she was always checking in with her father to see that he was on the straight and narrow.

Only after the meal would she tell him about the soy. She'd purchased some really good stuff that just might pull the wool over his eyes.

After she cooked for him, they ate, her father never complaining until she told him about the nonmeat.

"Phooey," he said, standing with his empty plate in hand.

"Love you," she said right back, wishing she could say it a thousand times to make up for all the days she'd grown up without him.

They cleaned up, watched some TV. Then she took his temperature, which was normal, and made sure he was comfortable in his bed before she walked back to the guesthouse.

When she arrived, she got ready to turn in right away, excited to jump onto the king-size luxury mattress with its silky sheets. Around her, original oils of vintage Parisian scenes decorated the walls, each one like a subliminal advertisement for happiness.

She wandered over to the gilded vanity table, unloading her beauty aids, then opening a passion fruit–scented lotion. Sniffing it, she closed her eyes, realizing that it smelled like a more sophisticated version of some old stuff that she'd used back when she was younger. The memory of the other scent took her back to days in the Texas sun, summer nights spent chasing fireflies and chancing secret, almost reluctantly admirable looks at Tyler while trying to capture their light in jars…

But there was a hint of the negative in those recollections, too. The night of The Situation. All the nights thereafter when her parents had slowly but surely stopped talking at the dinner table, her mom's resentment growing because her dad didn't have the "machismo" a man should have when another verbally beat him down. Then there was the time Zoe's father had taken her aside and told her that sometimes a man had to take one instance of a boss's bad mood because a good job was what kept a family eating, and that was all Poppy wanted to do— keep his family fed and clothed.

Zoe started to put the lotion away, but then she changed her mind. She'd gotten past everything about this ranch. She was where she wanted to be in life, and nothing could make her feel that vulnerable again.

She rubbed some lotion onto her arms, slipped into her lacy pajamas and then the amazing bed.

As she cuddled under the covers, she dreamed of swimming holes, rainbows under a summer rain shower and a young Tyler Barron laughing during hide-and-seek, all the while knowing she would have to wake up to reality in the morning.

That same night, Tyler walked out of the Longhorn Bar and Grill in town while a waning moon hung over Main Street. Festival trimmings flapped in a gentle wind while the fair's stragglers drove off in their cars.

He'd filled up on a steak and potatoes meal, but he still felt empty as he ambled toward the dirt lot where he'd parked the blue pickup he'd borrowed from the ranch. He didn't want to drive around in his Jag. Too flashy. Too...

Too much of a reminder of the city, of work and everything he'd left behind for a while, until he could get his head on straight.

It seemed unlikely that he would ever figure out just where his life had run off the rails. But he'd be damned if he didn't get it back on track. The thing would be to find some kind of purpose, because now that he'd taken a step back from the office to think, he'd realized that work hadn't been enough. Marriage hadn't been, either. And family...?

It had all been a lie for years.

The worst thing was that Tyler had allowed every bit of this to happen. He'd let his dedication to his family and The Group overshadow his life and even his marriage. And for what? The humiliation of having his father force him to step down from the one job Tyler had embraced over everything else, including the life he might have led if he'd followed his heart instead?

As a cowboy rode down the opposite side of the quiet street on his quarter horse filly, Tyler's heart clenched. What would things have been like if he'd pushed aside The Group and bought his own spread?

He watched the man and horse clomp into the distance, then went on his way.

As he passed boutiques closing up shop for the night, he tried to clear his mind, but another matter kept hounding him.

Zoe, the one who was going to make everything right.

I'm the scumbag your dad hired to clean up your family scandal.

Her words hadn't left him all day, and it wasn't just that she seemed to be the enemy right now.

It was *her.*

He couldn't stop thinking about how flames had seemed to lick the inside of his belly when he'd first seen Zoe, just before she'd told him her name. How his blood had surged with a primal attraction he hadn't felt in such a long time.

He'd felt that way when he'd first met Kristen back in college. But he'd been a kid then, and that first knock of attraction had been drawn out into years of dating during their time at Harvard Business School, then eventually marriage. Of course, then they'd fallen *out* of love.

Yet, with Zoe, there'd been a yank at his libido, a tug to his heart, and he didn't know what to do with those responses anymore.

But he sure knew what he *wouldn't* be doing—acting

on an impulse that would only spell trouble. He didn't know much right now, but at least he knew that he couldn't reconcile himself with anyone who didn't see the wrongness of what his dad and Aunt Laura had brought on the family.

He walked toward the fairgrounds, where the main lights were turning out, one by one, leaving dim, buttery flares of illumination from inside the tents and stray laughter from carnies who were drinking during their off hours. In the middle of it all, he heard a horse nickering near a trailer whose lights were out.

As he passed the structure, he spotted the animal tied to the side.

Their gazes connected, and Tyler stopped walking.

Maybe he was projecting, but he could've sworn that those big brown eyes echoed just what Tyler was feeling now. An aloofness from life. A…confusion.

But his fancifulness wore off real quick as his gaze traveled the rest of the male quarter horse, including its black hide, which seemed dull and lifeless, covering a body that looked ill fed. If he could've guessed, he would say this had once been a cutting horse—smaller with hindquarters that should've been powerful, not diminished.

The anger that rode so close to the surface of his skin threatened to flare up, but pity and sympathy pushed it down.

His throat tightened as he sank to a squatting position, making himself smaller in front of the horse, who warily stared at him.

Cautious. Unhappy. It wasn't right to make another creature feel that way.

"Hey, there," Tyler said softly.

The horse shied away. It didn't seem as if it would bolt exactly, but it wasn't trusting, that was for sure.

As Tyler waited the horse out, he found that the effort made him breathe easier. It made thoughts of his family fade a little, because this was more important right now.

At least it seemed that way.

Tyler didn't know how long he sat there, patient, in no rush, while he waited for the horse to show him a sign that it would welcome him.

But the wait paid off when the animal stepped toward him.

And, when Tyler didn't move, it came closer.

Finally, after what seemed like hours, the horse came near enough to nose him, then shy away.

Since it had his scent, Tyler felt confident in slowly raising his hand, offering the back of it for the horse to sniff.

It did, then nuzzled Tyler's hand again.

Tyler smiled.

But when the door to the trailer opened, the horse backed away to its original spot, far off.

A man walked out of the trailer, his hair disheveled, his voice slurred, and it wasn't because he'd been slumbering. Tyler could practically smell the cheap whiskey from here.

"What're you doin'?" the man drawled, buttoning the top of his jeans.

By now, the horse was almost hiding behind the trailer, the rope hanging down, swaying a little, even though the animal stood still.

Tyler told himself to breathe. If he didn't, he was going to lay into this guy. "This your horse?"

"Yeah."

"He hasn't been getting enough to eat."

"Like it's any of your business."

Red blasted over Tyler's vision, but he made himself sit tight, looking at that horse again.

If Tyler had just stayed away from The Group, horses would be nothing but his business. Especially the ones who needed the most help.

He wasn't sure, but he could've sworn he saw the animal peek out at him, as if wondering whether Tyler was going to leave.

Tyler bunched his hands into fists. Hell, no.

Without thinking of anything but what was right and just, he got out his wallet, took out a wad of cash—he didn't care how much—then dropped it at the foot of the stairs. He did it all very slowly, so as not to scare the horse.

The man's eyes went wide at the sight of the money.

Tyler made *shhh*ing sounds, approaching the horse again slowly, so slowly, offering his hand so the animal could smell him another time.

The animal rubbed against Tyler.

The man had come down the stairs by now, going for the money, unfolding it as if to count it right there and then. The horse stomped.

Tyler backed away, addressing the man while still watching the animal. He kept his voice quiet and level, even though he wanted to yell.

"Unless you want me to call the law so they can witness what you've been doing to him, you'll sign the registration papers and put them on those steps."

From what Tyler knew, nonprofit rescue organizations

had no right to seize mistreated animals without plenty of documentation and then even a civil case in court. But the man wasn't arguing. Not with the amount of money he'd gotten his hands on. He went back into his trailer, smiling as if he'd won a lottery with all the money that Tyler had given him.

The horse exhaled loudly.

He smiled again as he inched toward his new friend, finally feeling as if he would find whatever he'd left behind all those years ago when he'd given his heart and soul to The Group.

Zoe left her guesthouse early enough to catch her dad before he got out of bed. She cooked him another healthy breakfast—an egg-white omelet "without the good yellow part," he complained—then made sure he was relaxing with one of the model airplanes he liked to build as a hobby.

With her handheld camera in tow, she left to walk the ranch, scouting locations for the interviews that would take place after she leaked the scandal to a couple of carefully chosen reporters. She wanted the press to stay away from the corporate offices and the mansion. Instead, she would invite them to Barron country territory, where she could play down the family's cosmopolitan sheen and present them as people who were actually decent folk trying to work through their problems in private, as a family should. Her staff, including Ginnifer, would be working on TV and internet releases, too. Later today, the intern was going to come out here to take care of administrative details while Zoe brainstormed with her associates on a conference call from the office.

As she walked by the cabins, she filmed the humble homes, one of which housed the new foreman.

She found herself smiling at the thought of sitting on the steps of one, drinking a morning cup of tea, but…hey, didn't she have a much nicer guesthouse she'd worked her way up to?

After walking for about twenty minutes, past the new barn, past the corrals, then the old abandoned barn that she'd played in as a kid, she came to a pasture, where she discovered something so unexpected that she lowered the camera.

Tyler, leaning up against the outside of the fence while a skinny, coal-hued quarter horse nosed at the grass from way over on the opposite side. It looked as if the cowboy was giving the animal a lot of room.

And from the way he was training his gaze on the horse, it looked as if he was wearing his heart on his sleeve. There was something *simpatico* going on there, making this strong man seem vulnerable.

Zoe's skin came alive, as if every inch of it had caught fire. She even burned inside—languid, undulating waves of desire that had grown from a young girl's unwilling admiration into a woman's need—and one that was just as unwelcome.

But that was ridiculous. This was Tyler, the eldest Barron. His father had led the way in showing that they didn't stand for vulnerability, or even what she thought of as decency.

He must have sensed her presence, because he glanced over his shoulder, his cowboy hat shading his eyes, but not his mouth. No, that part was all too readable, with its straight line of displeasure.

Just as she was thinking about turning around and continuing on her way, he spoke.

"Morning walk?" he asked, keeping his voice low.

The first thing she realized was that he was being quiet because of the animal, who was probably skittish.

The second thing was that he was being…civil.

To her—the scumbag.

She nodded in response to his question, turning off the camera and putting the strap over her bare shoulder. Then she tugged down her sleeveless top in sudden awareness that maybe it was showing too much… shoulder. Not that it was particularly sexy, especially in the summer heat, but…

Well, she just felt aware of every inch of skin around him.

She nodded toward the horse. "He looks…"

"…unhealthy?" he finished for her in that murmur. "I noticed, too, last night when I found him."

"You…found him?" He talked as if he'd come upon a lucky penny. You didn't just *find* horses like that.

He shrugged, turning back to watch the animal, almost as if he didn't want her to see his expression. She walked closer, and his shoulders stiffened, so she stopped.

"Where did you find him?" she asked.

"The fair. Some carny had him tied to a trailer. God knows what he was using him for. At first I thought pony rides, but I think it might take some persuading for this horse to have people on and off his back all day. Even so, he'll come around to trusting again. He just seems a little warier today, in his new surroundings."

There was a bite of challenge in Tyler's voice, and

in a flash, Zoe saw past the vulnerability. Just as she'd thought: he'd grown up to be the mighty golden boy. Confident that he could dictate terms to a horse…and also to the world at large.

But it would be good to have him on her side during this campaign, so she stuck to her guns, refusing to back away like a cowed thing. A ranch rat.

She ran a compassionate gaze over the animal. "How could anyone do that to a…" She was about to say person, but instead, she said, "…horse?"

His jaw clenched. "I don't know, but I'm getting him care as soon as possible—a vet, a dentist, a farrier. There's a lot to be done."

Zoe could only look at Tyler. So was there a heart somewhere in that infamously corporate body?

She raised her camera to get some of this on film, thinking Tyler's good deed could potentially be part of the redemption of The Barron Group.

"No," Tyler said.

Even though she didn't like being commanded, he *had* made it clear that he didn't want anything to do with the PR campaign, so she lowered the camera.

"What's his name?" she asked, trying to keep the conversation going.

Tyler paused, as if trying to get a read on her tone, but he kept staring straight ahead. "I haven't come up with one yet, but I'm sure anything will be better than his old name. He'll be rechristened, like he's getting a second chance."

"How about that, then?" she said. "Chance?"

A smile crept over his mouth, and when her heart seemed to flutter, she fought the sensation.

"I like that," he finally said. "Chance."

They lapsed into silence as they watched the horse, who seemed perfectly content right now, under a morning sun that promised the wither of a Texas summer's day. Zoe moved a little nearer to Tyler, a couple feet away. It was actually nice, being out here, accompanied by memories of what she'd loved about the countryside before she'd left it.

As she took in the heavy scent of the grass, she also found notes of Tyler in there somewhere—that musky clean scent of a man who'd remained more in her memories than she'd ever admitted.

The boy running and laughing through the meadows during a game of tag…the boy who'd taken her breath away whenever he would chase her, touch her, saying, "You're it…"

She opened her eyes, the brightness suffusing the dimness of the past, and as her sight adjusted, she saw Tyler out of the corner of her gaze, watching her.

Zoe turned her head, catching his eyes under the shade of his hat, her heart pounding its way out of her chest.

For a moment, he appeared to forget his distaste for Zoe and her job as his gaze came to rest on her lips.

For a moment, nothing else mattered.

Chapter Three

Tyler's blood fizzed through his veins as he looked at the lush pink of Zoe's mouth, imagining what it would be like to close the distance between them and brush his lips against hers.

Would she inhale, surprised, before she closed her eyes and gave in?

Or would she push him away?

No doubt about that last option. She was here to work, not to cross a professional line. Same with him, although his line was more of the personal variety.

He hadn't been so good at personal commitment—marriage especially. And any woman who'd gone out with him in the past few years knew that he was the ultimate bachelor—unavailable and short-term, married to his job, just as his ex had said during all her justifications.

You were having an affair with work long before I started seeing someone outside our marriage.

Even though Tyler told himself to stop looking at Zoe's mouth, he took his time in pulling away his gaze. Just one more second of enjoying the allure of those soft lips. Just one more instant of imagining how her hair would feel sliding through his fingers as he cupped his hand over the back of her head, pulling her in for a deep kiss…

When Zoe bit her bottom lip, he blinked, glanced away to his new horse, who was eyeing the grass a few yards off.

Chance. That was his name—and that was just what Tyler had right now on the ranch. The chance to rebuild his own life, his future. And he wasn't going to blow any opportunities by making some kind of rash move on the PR woman.

He heard Zoe next to him, her breathing so even that he wondered if she was trying to control it in the wake of the intense moment. He tried to do the same to his jittering pulse.

But the awareness just kept hanging there, a misty screen between them.

"What's on today's PR agenda?" he said, ending the silence.

She sounded just as guarded. "I'm laying the ground-work for what's to come—tweaking an old Barron Group commercial so it'll lead in to the big media reveal, preparing to coach everyone for press interviews."

She was watching him now. His skin told him so, because it tingled.

He kept his gaze on Chance. "You like your job?"

When she hesitated, he got the feeling it was because she thought he was testing her.

He looked at Zoe straight on, but she'd already turned her sights to the horse. She wore a grin, showing a small dimple. Maybe there'd be one on the other side as well.

"You can talk about your job to me," he said. "I won't bite your head off."

"All right then, yes, I do like my job."

She leaned her arms on top of the fence, the camera still in her hand. She'd respected his wishes and wasn't filming Chance, though. He'd stopped her from doing so because being here with his horse had seemed like something new for him, something that hadn't been tainted by his previous mistakes. Chance really was a fresh opportunity, and Tyler didn't want to drag him into everything that had come before.

"My job," she said, "even allows me to see where you're coming from, Tyler. That's a part of what I do—I look at things from the angles of everyone involved. The stakes are high because I deal with people's lives, their businesses, their reputations, and saving those makes my career worthwhile. That's why I like it. It's a challenge, too—like trying to rearrange pieces of a puzzle in a way that creates a nicer picture than was first presented."

"A picture that reinterprets the real situation?" Like a puzzle that was originally supposed to show the oil portrait in the lounge, with Eli, Florence, Tyler and Jeremiah? Did she want to rearrange that to show Chet, too, as the family sat on their front porch, sipping lemonade and smiling at each other?

"You still think it's wrong to do a shine job on your family," she said, her voice tight.

At her tone, something fell inside Tyler's chest, but he didn't know why. He'd lost his heart a long time ago with Kristen and, right now, he was all the better for it. At least he could thank his ex-wife for that—saving him the pain of getting his heart broken ever again.

She sighed. "I guess it wouldn't matter if I mentioned that, in the past, some good PR work has eased a few other situations for the Barrons."

"Are you talking about what happened with my ex?" he asked.

"Yes. I haven't seen the files, but I heard another PR firm kept the most salacious parts of the story under wraps."

He wondered just how much she knew about his wife's infidelities. Eli hadn't wanted Kristen's betrayals to sully the Barron image, so that was why everything had been so hush-hush about the divorce.

Zoe must've sensed that he wasn't about to expand on that topic, so she changed the subject. "I can definitely help you in this case. Even if you think that the public has no business nosing around in this, either, Chet's introduction into your family affects The Barron Group. Stockholders and clients will feel that they have a right to know what's going to happen with the new dynamics…and what *did* happen previously."

"I know." He hated to admit that she was right, but she was.

He'd started leaning on the fence, too, echoing her posture, but even after realizing it, he didn't straighten up. This was actually peaceful—a summer's morning, a horse wandering, a breeze on his face. And Zoe's heady scent, which smelled like exotic, tempting fruit.

"Back when you lived here," he said, "did you ever think you'd be doing this?"

"What—talking you out of despising me?"

He couldn't hold back a surprised laugh. "No. Did you think you'd be in a high-powered job that ties in with the Barrons in such a way?"

There went that little grin on her mouth, and it did something to Tyler's insides—scrambled them. Made them go upside down in a way that a corporate shark should be able to control with ease.

"I did think I'd end up doing something important with my life," she said. "I knew early on that I was going to succeed at whatever I chose, too. I suppose you could even say your family inspired me."

"How?"

She grinned again, as if she didn't want to tell him.

"Just say it," he said.

"Okay. I thought your family had it pretty good, and I hoped I could have the same. You all made me completely buy in to the pursuit of the American dream." Her tone changed, going taut again. Envy? "I saw your mansion, your fancy schools…"

She was painting a picture that made him tense up, too. He didn't remember any of the ranch kids hating him or Jeremiah. He just recalled days at the swimming hole, splashing around with them. Games in the barn and the meadows before his parents found out and put an end to the fun.

But had he ever taken the time to get to know any of them?

Now that Tyler thought about it, maybe he'd seen the

kids as just being another part of the ranch—as if they came with the horses and fences and stables.

He'd never really known Zoe was around. Not until now.

She straightened her posture, as if she'd caught herself going down a path she hadn't meant to. "Anyway, I was definitely going to make it big someday. Even my dad's proud of what I've accomplished."

She stiff-armed the fence, giving Tyler the impression that maybe she regretted bringing up her dad in front of him.

"Dads are funny," he said. "I don't know if it's the same for a daughter as it is for a son, but—"

"It's probably not the same."

She was fiddling with her camera, as if she was thinking about putting an end to the personal talk. Ironic that she knew his business but he didn't know hers.

Not that he could help anyone manage *their* business, anyway.

"How's your dad doing?" he asked. "I hear he was sick."

"He's fine, just slower to move than usual, but not too lacking in energy to complain about my cooking."

She smiled, but there was a hint of pain there. Maybe it wasn't as dramatic as what the Barrons had gone through with Eli, but Tyler knew it when he saw it, and he suspected it had something to do with how her own family had been broken way back when.

"Not to say I'm a bad cook, you understand," she added. "My dad just doesn't like that I'm foisting healthy stuff on him."

"Sounds like a regular father to me. Whether it's a son or daughter, there'll be some complaining."

"Right." She pointed in the direction of the stables. "I've got to get going."

And he watched her leave, enjoying the sway of her hips and the way her white pants cupped her rear end. Desire warmed him and, for a fleeting moment, he imagined Zoe in jeans, just like all ranch dwellers.

What would she have turned out to be if she'd stayed on the ranch? He liked how she'd grown up—no doubt about that—but he liked the idea of down-home Zoe, too.

As Tyler turned back to Chance, he thought again about what his life would've been like had he stayed a cowboy, with his own land stretching around him...

...and his very own cowgirl.

After Tyler spent the day with the vet, the farrier and the veterinary dentist—all of whom he'd paid quite a bit of money to come out and see Chance on an urgent basis—he showered and checked on Uncle Abe in the big house.

Abe was awake when Tyler entered a downstairs guestroom distinguished by its French windows, which let in a spill of sunlight. Tyler had thought the illumination might cheer his uncle.

"Why, if it isn't Wild Bill," Uncle Abe said after getting a gander at Tyler's jeans, boots and striped Western shirt. "No one in the office would recognize you."

It was obviously a great day for his uncle, and his male nurse, Johnny, grinned at Tyler while settling down in a chair to do a crossword puzzle.

Tyler tried to ignore Abe's sparse, shockingly thin gray hair and parchment skin as he sat next to him. His uncle's prostate cancer had metastasized, and they were doing everything possible to keep him comfortable during his chemo treatments. That was why it had been unthinkable for all this drama to have gone down, and then for Eli to desert the ranch without standing by Abe's side, caring for his brother.

Unlike his dad, Tyler sat with Abe for the next hour, telling his uncle about the county fair, which he'd visited at Abe's request. Otherwise he would've just stayed away.

"Did you get me any goodies?" Abe asked.

Johnny spoke up. "Eh, eh, Mr. Barron."

Tyler hid a smile. "I don't think funnel cakes and cotton candy fit into your diet plan."

"Only in paradise." The man sighed and looked toward the window.

All right. Obviously the light part of the conversation had passed them by.

"Now that matters have settled down," Abe said, "I want to make sure you're not going to crucify Eli when he gets back."

Tyler hadn't broached the subject with his uncle since that night. He'd been afraid for Abe's health and state of mind. But now that the topic was as large as an elephant in the room, the anger Tyler had pushed far down into himself threatened to surge right back up.

It was all too easy to put himself in Abe's place, shoved to the fringes of the Barron family.

Johnny, the nurse, lifted his gaze from the crossword, monitoring Abe, and Tyler calmed himself.

"You've forgiven my dad?" he asked his uncle.

Abe rested his head back against the wicker chair. "I realized I'd need to do that a long time ago, when Laura confessed the affair to me. I forgave both of them because living with bitterness punished me more than it did them. Besides, Laura made up for it every day afterward. I believed her when she told me that it was a short, ill-advised fling she didn't think her way through. She was the best of wives after that."

Tyler knew too well about wives who strayed, and all he could do was sit there in silence. It was even worse realizing that his uncle had been privy to Eli and Laura's affair all this time—that he'd accepted Chet as his own son, even as he'd worked with Eli every day.

It took quite a man to withstand such a storm. A brave one.

"Did my mom know?" Tyler asked.

"About Laura, or about Eli's other affairs?"

"You know what I mean."

His uncle paused, then slowly shook his head. "God bless Florence, but I'm pretty sure she didn't realize a thing. Eli refused to tell her, and Laura kept the secret, too. Then again, your mom had a way of turning the other cheek when it came to Eli."

Tyler leaned his forearms on his thighs. Should he be happy that his mother was unaware? Maybe ignorance *was* bliss.

"The forgiving must've been hard for you," he said.

"Yes, but I never *forgot*."

His uncle's voice had an edge to it, and Tyler slowly sat up as Abe added, "That's why I asked Eli to tell the family about his relationship with Chet the other night."

Why did it sound like Abe really hadn't left all the bad feelings behind? That his talk of forgiveness was only a cover, and he was still holding on to some bitterness, after all?

"*You* told my dad to make the announcement?" Tyler asked.

Abe closed his watery eyes, opened them. "Yes. Chet and I weren't on good terms for a long time. He was up in Montana when I thought he should've been down here, and that stung me. Then I got sick, and when I started to accept what was happening to my body, I told Eli it was time to bring Chet into his proper family. I said, 'Make sure he's well provided for,' and I didn't mean that Chet should be stuck on that cattle ranch of his. I wanted him to have his share of The Group—his rightful portion. So we brought him here, let him get to know you and Jeremiah. Then it was only a matter of my health improving enough so that I'd be up to telling him the truth."

Anger still gnawed at Tyler, just below his skin, but he couldn't give in to it. Abe was preparing them all, especially Chet, for his death.

His uncle—the man who always burst into a genuine smile when he saw Tyler. The mentor who always had time for him, who encouraged him even during the darkest of days.

Dying.

Heaviness stole over Tyler, weighing him down.

His uncle's voice regained its edge. "Before I pass on, I wanted to be assured that your dad faced the consequences. And I wanted to ask you and Jeremiah to make sure Chet really became your brother. I especially want *you* to let me know that's going to happen, Ty."

As always, Abe looked on him with pure faith and

pride in his gaze. A belief that his nephew would never let him down.

Then he leaned forward and put his hand on Tyler's. "Promise me?"

Tyler couldn't do anything but nod, even though it wasn't in him to welcome Chet into anything right now. Hell, he knew full well that his anger at Chet was misplaced, since the man was a victim, as well, but Chet was a symbol of all that his father had ever gotten away with—a sign of hubris and irresponsibility.

Yet Chet was his half brother, too.

Abe squeezed Tyler's hand, but it was a weak gesture. Still, he must've been content for now, because he closed his eyes, the sunlight brushing over his wan skin.

Before Tyler knew it, his uncle had drifted off to sleep.

As he rose to go, Tyler grabbed a quilted comforter from the bed, tucking it around Uncle Abe, then stood back. It hadn't been all that long ago that Abe had looked like a brown-eyed version of Eli and Chet, with the same thick, dark blond hair and boxer's body. It hadn't been long ago that Uncle Abe had been the best two-stepper around, raising hell on dance floors all over the county.

Everything had been different not long ago.

He started to leave the room, avoiding the empathetic smile that Johnny offered.

In spite of all Abe had told him, Tyler kept repeating that his uncle had enjoyed a good day, free of pain and discomfort. And that was what was important, wasn't it?

But as he walked to the cabins, he damned his father, anyway.

When Eli Barron got back into town, there'd be a lot to answer for.

* * *

It seemed to take the entire night to get to his temporary home, but when Tyler came to the pine trees that shaded the first of the cabins—Keith the foreman's—he found the guy outside, barbecuing on a grill. Rosemary-tinged smoke drifted on the air as Keith waved Tyler over.

"What're you doing for dinner?" he asked. His cowboy hat hid most of his straw-colored hair, but his brown eyes were in full view, flashing with good humor. He often invited the hands for meals, and Tyler had already eaten with him once.

"I hadn't really thought about what's in store for me tonight." He barely knew what was in his refrigerator, but that was why God had invented the Longhorn Bar and Grill in town. He hadn't even been aware that he was hungry, to tell the truth.

"How does steak sound?"

His stomach gave a rumble, as if arguing with the emotions that had cut off his appetite. Maybe the best thing for him right now *was* to sit with Keith, drink a beer, relax a little and slowly absorb what Abe had told him.

"A steak sounds pretty damn good," he said.

Keith gestured toward his cabin. "I've got master cooks inside, working on some kind of secret marinade. How do you like your beef?"

"Rare."

"Got it." Keith bent down, extracted a bottle of beer from an ice chest and tossed it to Tyler.

Assuming that some of the hands would be doubling as the master cooks, he sat on the bench at Keith's long table. It was decorated with tin plates and paper napkins weighed down by tarnished forks and knives.

Tyler was used to polished silver and candlelight, but the sight of a simple table did something to him. Made him smile, even a bit. And he needed a smile.

When he heard a woman's laughter from inside Keith's cabin, he glanced over, knowing who was going to come out before she appeared.

Miguel Velez opened the screen door, holding it for his daughter while he carried a bowl of corn on the cob in the other hand. As Zoe passed him, she balanced a large platter of steaks.

She'd changed into a white sundress that made her look like an angel from the prairie. She'd even pulled her brown hair back into a soft, flipped-up ponytail at her nape, and it left her neck in full view, long and slender, the skin so smooth that Tyler's fingertips itched to touch it.

His pulse kicked as she looked over to find him at the table. When their gazes met, his groin tightened.

All he saw was what life should be—simple, uncomplicated. Zoe in her white dress.

But in the next click of a second, Tyler saw the enemy—the woman who was here to erase his father's betrayal.

He almost got up to leave, but after a strained moment, he stayed put.

What was he going to do every time he saw Zoe? Run?

It was time he faced up to everything—the reasons for his anger, the way he'd turned aside from what life should've been for him.

He wasn't going anywhere.

Keith asked Zoe to bring over the steaks and, tearing her gaze away from Tyler—was she giving him a scrutinizing look?—she went down the steps to the foreman. He whisked the platter away from her then slapped the meat on the grill.

Miguel made his way over to Tyler, who stood to shake his hand.

"Good to see you," the older man said, easing himself down to the opposite bench.

It wasn't as if they'd ever visited much, whenever Tyler made it to the ranch.

"Likewise," he said to Miguel, all the while trying not to eyeball the man's daughter by the grill.

Did she have to be over there with Keith? And what were they saying to each other?

Jealousy wasn't a familiar emotion to Tyler, and he shrugged it off.

He wasn't jealous—just keeping the PR woman in his sights. That was all.

He turned back to Miguel, finally noticing how the man seemed to have gotten older, even though he wasn't all that advanced in years. Merely slower, as Zoe had said.

As Tyler was about to start thinking about Abe again, Zoe called out that she needed to get the rest of the side dishes, and she disappeared into Keith's cabin.

Tyler looked after her, then returned his attention to the present company, only to find Miguel watching him, a slight lift to one of his heavy brows.

But he didn't say anything as he pushed the corn on the cob toward Tyler, who was only too glad to occupy himself.

Zoe was out within a minute, first bearing a tray with

a big plastic container of salad, a ceramic bowl of baked beans and a basket of fresh bread that was still warm to the touch. Then she went back inside, emerging with another place setting.

The homey smell of baked goods blanketed Tyler through and through.

"Bread machine," Miguel said. "Zoe bought one for me, and I brought it over here tonight to give it a test run."

"It's an Amish wheat mix." Zoe put a small piece of bread on her dad's plate. "It's good for you."

Miguel looked at Tyler. "She takes care of me, this one, even better than I can take care of her."

The comment seemed saturated in hard feelings— Tyler could tell from the way Zoe just kept putting things on her dad's plate without answering.

Keith arrived with the steaks, using tongs to set them down on everyone's plate but Zoe's. She was loading her and her father's plate with mostly side dishes.

Keith saw this, too. "Where's your protein, girl?"

She pointed to the beans.

Miguel said, "She put some soy crap in there."

"Thanks, Dad. No one would've noticed." She appealed to Keith. "It has the texture of crumbled beef."

Tyler took a big scoop of the beans and ate them. They weren't bad at all. Good, as a matter of fact.

His pleasure must've shown, because Zoe smiled slightly at him, yet when he caught her, she looked away.

"Come on, Miguel," Keith said. "Just give those beans a try."

Between mouthfuls, the foreman engaged his guests in small talk, expertly avoiding the pitfalls of any awkward topics. Tyler appreciated that, as well as the beer and hearty food.

But being able to see Zoe so clearly allowed him to catch a few moments of subtle tension between her and her dad: it was more in the way they didn't talk right now unless they had to, and Tyler suspected that had something to do with the comment Miguel had made about her taking care of him better than he took care of her.

Bit by bit, he started to recall scraps of gossip from the ranch, not that he'd ever paid a lot of mind to it. Now that he was really thinking, though, he remembered something about Miguel's wife leaving in a huff and how that might've had something to do with Tyler's own dad…

After the meal, Miguel wanted to smoke a cigar with Keith, but Zoe nixed that idea.

"Poppy," she said, "weren't you the one with pneumonia not too long ago?"

"Phooey," the older man said. But he said it in a way that made Tyler think he kind of liked being looked after, even if he complained.

Miguel insisted on going back to his nearby cabin on his own, and Tyler could tell that Zoe thought her dad was pouting.

"Okay, then, sweet dreams," she said to him, standing on her tiptoes and kissing her dad on the cheek.

Then she turned to Keith. "I'll get things cleaned up and then be off to my place."

"I'll help," Tyler said.

"No, no, no," the foreman said. "I've got it under control. Scoot, y'all."

There was no arguing, so they thanked Keith while

Miguel ambled toward his own cabin, a mere hundred feet away. In the other little homes, the lights burned in the night.

He and Zoe just stood there, knowing full well that his cabin was on the way to hers.

But dinner with her hadn't been a total disaster. He could walk her partway to her cottage now without the world exploding.

He jerked his chin in the direction they'd both be going, and she seemed to get the message.

They walked through the pines, the needles crunching under their feet. Just in case she made something more of his gesture, he added, "I'm going to check on Chance, anyway."

"Well, I appreciate the company."

They moved out of the pines and through the moonlight-drenched grass until they got to a gravel path that led to the main grounds. As the crickets sang, he could feel Zoe's warmth from her bare arms, even through his long shirtsleeves. It practically breathed through him.

"I talked to Chet today," she said, as if wanting to break the silence, just as he'd done earlier today when they were with Chance. "He's coming back soon, after he finishes some work at his development project in Utah."

"I thought he might not stay away long."

He felt her measuring him up, as if she was trying to figure out just what he thought about Chet. His new brother.

Through everything, this one fact hadn't really hit him until tonight, but there it was, waiting for him to latch on to it.

He couldn't though. Not yet.

"It's rough," he said, a little startled to hear that he was talking to her, "thinking things are one way in life when they turn out to be another. It's as if I stepped into a parallel universe, where things are mostly the same, but not."

"I get that. You sort of feel like you're floating, that things are going to eventually come back down into their proper places, but they never do. That's how I felt when my parents separated."

He thought back to dinner, to what he'd seen between her and Miguel.

Tyler frowned. Since when had *he* become so astute about people—and not just in a business way, either?

Could it be that just being here, living away from the mansion and the city, had given him a little perspective? Could it be that he'd needed to come back to the ranch to find this, and to really understand what she was saying…?

She went on. "Even just a parental separation has a strong effect on a person."

"Why did they divorce?" he asked, wishing right away that he hadn't. But for some reason, he was interested.

"You really don't know?"

"I heard whisperings."

She sighed. "You're not going to want to hear about it."

Why not? He'd heard an earful tonight from Abe. After that, anything else would be peanuts.

He stopped walking altogether, and the motion accidentally made his arm brush against hers. An electric pulse zapped him just as she took in a small breath.

Had she felt it, too?

"Go ahead," he said, recovering.

When she looked up at him with those wide eyes, Tyler's chest seemed to open. But strangely, for the first time in weeks, he didn't slam himself shut again.

Chapter Four

It could've been the moonlight, with him standing over her, close enough to touch. It could've even been in the way he'd looked at her this morning, with his gaze devouring her mouth, as if he'd been thinking about kissing her. Either way, Zoe wasn't leaving.

Hard feelings—about his father, about her own dad— pounded at her, as if they were in a rush to get out, so she tempered her words.

"You could say my family always felt a tad second-class here, working for the Barrons."

Tyler seemed as if he was about to dispute that.

"But," she said, "that kind of dynamic is only natural. The Barrons are the bosses on their ranch." She took a handful of her skirt, frustrated, because she wasn't really saying what she wanted to. "I'm going to be absolutely truthful, Tyler."

His shoulders lost a little of their stiffness. It was as if he was tired of being angry, and he was finally allowing himself to let it go long enough to hear her out.

"It's your father," she finally said. "He believes in his absolute superiority, and I'm not only talking about him being high class. I know he valued my dad—he always called him the best foreman in the state—but there was one time Eli showed another side of himself. Just for a moment. I'm sure he regretted even saying what he said, although he never apologized for it."

"What did he say?"

She wished she didn't have to see this kind of exhaustion in him, to hear it in his voice, so she fought back her suppressed need to find a catharsis.

But he was a Barron, and it was tough not to remember that.

"One day Eli got angry about some fallen fences after a storm," she said. "My dad was aware of them, of course, but he apparently didn't get to them soon enough. In front of a group of hands, Eli called my dad a lazy, good-for-nothing Mexican, and said that unless he got the fences fixed lickety-split, he'd be a lazy, good-for-nothing unemployed Mexican."

Tyler crossed his arms over his chest, as if he could keep Eli's words away from him, too. She'd expected aggressive defensiveness—not this quiet deflection.

Had she been wrong about Tyler being just as cruel and knee-jerk careless as his dad?

"God, Zoe…"

"Don't apologize for him."

What *was* she searching for then, coming back here after all these years, if not for an apology?

As if trying to find out, she continued. "Eli acted like nothing had ever happened. Ultimately, he was happy with the fence mending and how quickly it was done, but the real trouble came when my mom heard the hands' wives talking about it. She was mortified, and she couldn't let it go. She told my dad to speak to Eli and stand up to him like a real man, but he thought it was prudent to keep the peace. Everything had already blown over, he said, so why stir it up again? She argued that self-worth and pride were more valuable than a paycheck."

"Sometimes they are." There was that world weariness again.

Zoe looked into his eyes, but he wasn't showing her anything he didn't want to. "As you can imagine, my dad didn't see it the same way as my mom. Maybe because a man takes great stock in providing for his family, and he was dead-set on keeping the money coming in. Being foreman is a good job, and quitting it seemed too risky, so he was willing to let it ride unless Eli slighted him again—which he didn't. But that didn't matter to Mom. The whole thing changed how she thought of my dad, and nothing was the same after that."

Zoe paused, but Tyler was still listening.

Listening to her like no one else had ever done before.

"My mom kept saying that the Barrons were arrogant," she added, "and she couldn't stand to live on their property as an inferior. But even though Eli never apologized, he gave my dad a huge raise and praised him to kingdom come. That was apology enough for him. Still, my mom resented that he wouldn't stand up for himself, even if it would've meant trouble. It seems like such a small incident, but it festered, and she filed for divorce and got custody of me, because she wanted to raise me in a place where she thought my self-esteem wouldn't suffer. She didn't want me to grow up thinking I was lower class, and my dad let us both go, because, somewhere deep down, I'm afraid he thought she was right." By now, she felt deflated, but better. A lot better. "I even think my dad *believes* what Eli said about him—to some extent—even though that sounds ridiculous."

Tyler was really watching her now, so intently that it seemed as if, any second, he would touch her arm, silently telling her that everything was good between them—the daughter of Miguel and the son of Eli. The remnants of an earlier fallout.

She wished he *would* reach out. But he shouldn't. It would just make it harder to prove to everyone here on Florence Ranch that she would never take what Eli had dished out to her father.

Maybe *that* was what she'd come here looking for.

"The whole thing must have been tough," he said, resting his hands on his hips, not trying to touch her at all.

In fact, she detected some pity, and something stirred in her.

Barron pity.

"I dealt with it," she said, and although she didn't mean for it to happen, she raised her chin a notch. "I realized through the years that my parents would never be a couple again. That's what I meant by how the world seems to float because, for a while, I had these high-drifting fantasies that they would get back together. But when things came back down to earth, it turned out that my mom and dad were their own people with their own lives, and things were never going to go back to the way they were."

And then she'd turned to work, just as Tyler had done after his own divorce, according to the gossips. She'd buried herself in school, community activities, college, then the office, as if that was the best way to mend a broken heart.

But the truth was that, because of the divorce, she'd learned that it might not be worth opening herself to anyone. She'd dated now and then, whenever she had the time, but there'd always been some flaw in those men. Even if she had found the perfect guy for her—someone grounded, someone who knew just who he was and was so comfortable with himself that she wouldn't be able to resist feeling the exact same way around him, too—Zoe doubted she would've pursued anything with him.

Now there was a quality to Tyler's gaze that unsettled her. It was almost as if that weight he'd been carrying on his shoulders had taken up residence in him now, too. As if he was thinking that his family had created much more damage outside of his own brood than he'd ever suspected.

"My father is a bastard," he finally said. "And if there's anything I could do to make up for that, I sure as hell would."

What was behind those words? It was something she couldn't identify. Something that she knew would pull her even closer to him, and she couldn't afford that.

"Thanks for the thought, Tyler." She backed up, began to walk toward the guesthouse. "But I've got this under control."

And she left him standing alone, every step she took making her realize this was always how Tyler seemed to end up—alone.

Except *she'd* been the one to walk away this time.

* * *

In her guesthouse, Zoe tried to watch some TV, but it didn't hold her attention in the least. She even tried to lose herself in her laptop computer, hoping it would take her away, just as bubble baths seemed to do for luckier, less high-strung people, but...

Nope.

Funny, how she'd always called the Barrons arrogant. She'd lumped Tyler and Jeremiah with their father a long time ago, never really knowing them. *She* had been arrogant in doing that, and tonight had been no exception.

She had that chip on her shoulder, daring someone like Tyler to come along and knock it off, and when he hadn't, she'd shut him out.

It wasn't right, the way she'd laid all her frustrations about his family out on him. She'd grown up to be what she'd disliked most about the Barrons. Besides, this wasn't exactly the way to encourage a wonderful working relationship with Tyler, to persuade him to participate in the PR campaign.

She slipped on her sandals and took the path toward the pasture, the night air still warm. He'd said he would be checking on Chance, so she might be able to clear the air with him before things festered.

Would he still be there?

Moonlight illuminated the path, a patch of wildflowers, the pastures...and the movement she saw by the fence where she'd met Tyler this morning, when he'd been watching his new horse.

Seeing him there again, Zoe held a hand to her stomach. It had gone topsy-turvy, just as it always did around him.

He'd hooked an electric lantern on the fence post, and the light splashed over him, as if embracing him while he knelt on the ground inside the pasture, opposite where Chance was grazing.

He was gradually getting closer to his horse in the pasture. Not forcing himself on Chance, just getting the animal used to his presence.

Zoe didn't move, either. Tyler seemed so at peace right now, focused on his goal of getting that horse to accept him. Looking as if he'd finally come upon a place he belonged. She wouldn't dare break that.

When Tyler inched farther over the grass, moment by agonizing moment, Chance raised his head and looked at his new owner.

For a full minute, neither horse nor man moved. There was just Tyler, an obvious yearning to help Chance in the set of his body. There were just the sounds of night, the rustle of nearby cedar and oak leaves, even the sounds of frogs by the creek.

Then Tyler started to move forward again, but this time, Chance took a step backward.

Even such a subtle motion made Zoe think that she saw Tyler's shoulders sink, as if that much more of a strain had been put on him. All she wanted to do was ease his burden in some way.

But hadn't she vowed to do that already, by wrangling this family scandal?

Right now, it just didn't seem to be enough.

In the pasture, Chance made his way toward the shelter, and Tyler returned to the fence in his own time, eventually extinguishing the lantern, never even knowing that Zoe was there watching as he climbed the fence and landed on the other side with such rugged grace that her heart stumbled in its beat-beat-beating.

If she went to him, he would probably just blow her off, especially since she'd seen Chance reject him. So she stayed to the shadows as Tyler sauntered toward the cabins.

Full circle, Zoe thought. Because it was just like hide-and-seek all over again when they were young: with her staying out of sight, allowing just a peek to show from behind a stall in the old barn.

Meanwhile, Tyler never even saw her as he went in the opposite direction.

When Tyler woke up, he went straight to the laughing place, just as he'd been doing nearly every morning over the past week.

That was what they called the swimming hole—"the laughin' place." It had been that way for years. Tales had it that some old ranch hand or other had been a real storyteller, entertaining the ranch kids with everything from the adventures of Brer Rabbit to Jim Bowie. Kids being kids, they'd never thought about things like political correctness or history until much later, long after they outgrew swinging on the rope that extended from the branch of an oak.

As Tyler tossed his towel on the old deck, he took in the peace of a sun barely peeking over the cypresses, the limestone outcroppings, the little fern-strewn waterfall that fed the pool with springwater.

None of the ranch kids were here—most of them preferred the manmade pool and clubhouse that the Barrons had installed a few years ago near the cabins.

There was a widescreen TV and ice machine up there, along with a slide and lawn chairs.

Their loss, he thought. Then again, hadn't he left the simple life of the ranch for flashier things, too?

But he was back, wearing old swim trunks. He dove in, the water cool and all-encompassing as he pushed through it, falling into a rhythmic pattern of strokes while getting the exercise he'd been missing from his daily workout at the office gym.

But this was better.

Silent.

Perfect.

He stopped beneath the waterfall, letting the bracing water sluice over him. It was only when he finally came out from under it that everything rushed back to him, as if there was no escape at all.

His family. His future. Zoe.

Last night had never really left him. Besides Abe's confessions, Tyler kept mulling over those shadows he'd seen in Zoe's gaze when she'd talked about Eli and his big, egotistical mouth.

Surely there had to be a way to make it up to her. Then he would take on his *own* family...

He dove back into the water, swimming like hell until his breath ran out and he broke the surface, whipping the hair out of his eyes with one jerk of his head, then running a hand over his face as he treaded water.

When he saw Zoe standing on the deck, he didn't think she was real at first—that his conscience was hounding him and putting images where they shouldn't be.

So he wiped the water off his face again.

But she didn't go anywhere; she just kept standing

on that deck in sandals, cutoff jeans that showed her slender, tanned legs and a short, white T-shirt that clung to her curves.

Damn, did she have a lot of curves that she managed to hide under her business-casual clothes...

"I was taking a walk when I saw my dad and Keith," Zoe said. "They said you like to come out here some mornings."

He cut through the water, swimming to a spot where he could stand. In the background, the waterfall murmured.

So Zoe had been looking for him. The notion heated him up, right where he shouldn't have been heating.

"And why would you be searching me out?" he asked.

"It's about last night...I said some things that could've been held back." She shook her head. "I'm trying to let go of it all, you know? The bitterness. Besides business, that's one reason I returned to the ranch and my dad. But it all came out with you, anyway."

"Don't worry about it." He was trying to dismiss it all, but the words came out flat.

"I do worry. It's just that forgiveness takes work, and I'm doing everything I can to get there. That's why I'm sorry for how I talked to you."

Hadn't Abe said something similar about forgiving and forgetting? The difference was that his uncle didn't seem to want to forgive, no matter what he said. Hell, Abe was even putting Eli through the paces, making sure his brother made everything up to Chet.

And shouldn't they *all* be asking that of Eli?

Again, the anger for everything his dad had taken away simmered in Tyler. His dad had led him down one path—the business, the promise of a happy family—only to yank all of it away.

But that wasn't the worst part, was it?

The water dripped from Tyler, hitting the pool below him. He was the angriest at himself. He'd chosen to be the son Eli had wanted. He'd followed blindly, like a damn fool.

Did it make sense that he would have to forgive himself, right along with Eli?

As Tyler watched Zoe standing there, he wondered if this would be the first step—to accept *her* apology. To forgive and forget bit by bit until he learned how to do it.

She was twisting the bottom of her T-shirt and, for a second, her grown-up facade melted away, revealing someone far more vulnerable than the PR whirlwind who'd come into his life so suddenly after all these years. He saw the country girl underneath it all—her dark brown hair loose and unstyled right now, no makeup, no pretenses.

Someone so appealing that his body just about cried out for her.

"Thanks, Zoe," he said. "Thanks for coming down here and saying that."

It seemed as if something had changed between them. As if they'd cleared the air somewhat. He could see it in the way she stopped twisting her T-shirt, in how she offered a smile to him.

Another truce.

He ducked beneath the surface, coming up closer to the deck, then flicked the water off him again.

She shielded herself with her hands. "Hey!"

A trill of amusement laced her voice, and that changed the tone between them, too.

"Hey, what?" he said, going along with the moment.

"Hey, I don't have time for a dip. I've got to get ready for the film crew to come out. We'll be writing some scripts—questions that we'll go over with the family so they can rehearse for the press. The crew's going to wander around with their cameras, too, checking out places I've recommended and refilming them."

He parted the water, coming even closer to the deck.

Zoe backed up. "When you were younger, you used to come down here and play sea monster. You'd grab unsuspecting people on the deck and haul them in. Don't think I can't remember all that."

"Why would I do a thing like that now?"

He grinned, grabbing the deck and hauling himself up, resting his arms on it. Water dripped to the wood, which warmed his skin under the morning sun.

Yeah, the cleared air was much easier to breathe than the tense atmosphere that had strained their interactions before. He hadn't known just how sick he was of that tension until now.

"You've got goose bumps," she said.

And, indeed, he did. With her only about a foot away, he was getting a lot more than that, too.

The stirring in his belly whipped up his libido, making him reckless, forgetting his place...and hers.

"You were on a walk," he said. "Why not end it with a swim?"

"Nope."

"What, are you going to melt with a little water on you?"

She started to back up.

An impulsiveness he hadn't felt in…years?…got him in its clutches and he reached out, grabbed an ankle, then tugged her forward.

"Tyler, I'm serious—"

He heard her laughing in surprised reluctance as he got all the way onto the deck and, whip-quick, wrapped his arm around her waist, falling back into the water so he would take the brunt of the impact.

"Tyler!" she squealed, digging her nails into his forearms just before they splashed into the swimming hole.

They went under, burbles of sound…the silence of being submerged…her silky hair tickling his face as he held on just a second longer, then let her go.

They resurfaced at the same time, the world crashing back with a thrust of droplets and color.

A bigger splash hit Tyler after Zoe pushed water at him, then swam back toward the deck.

"It's cold!" she said, but she didn't sound angry. She was laughing too much.

He came after her again, laughing, too. Instead of levering herself up to the deck, she swam to the bank, where the water would be shallower. He'd forgotten that she was such a fast swimmer. Or maybe he'd never even known.

He caught her in his arms before she got too far, turned her around to face him. She pushed against his chest, breathing hard, still laughing, her dark hair raining water over them.

Panting, too, he held her waist, leaving her just above the waterline.

Her white T-shirt was soaked through, clinging to her dusky curves. He could make out the toned lines of her stomach, the flowery lace pattern of her bra. Could even see a hint of darkness where her nipples had gone hard.

He should've let her down right then, but he kept holding her up, his heart slamming, begging him to either stop looking or release her.

Her nails dug into his shoulders, as if urging him to do more than just stand there while the water dripped. It seemed to be the only sound, because even the birds had gone silent.

Off-limits, he thought, even as he felt the heat of her under his hands. *Just let her go.*

And he did let go, although he couldn't help doing it slowly, allowing her to slide back down into the water. Her legs clamped to the sides of him, slipping down his thighs, to the backs of his knees. She clamped around him, pressing against his belly, just above the erection that was starting to nudge his fly.

She reached up to push a hank of hair away from her face, and he saw it in the blue-gray of those eyes—the same desire he was struggling with.

The same doubts about this being a good idea.

The birds started up again, breaking the quiet. She laughed awkwardly and sent a wedge of water at him.

"Great," she said. "I didn't bring a towel."

"Just use mine, Miss High-Maintenance." He didn't know what else to say...or do.

"I'm not high-maintenance." Even as she said it, she seemed taken aback that he would think of her that way—so different from how she used to be on this ranch.

She sent one last splash his way, then swam to the deck, using a ladder to get to the platform. Once she was there, she pulled her shirt away from her chest, depriving him of that sumptuous view of her breasts, the hard, dark pink of her nipples…

Making a grab for his towel, she put on a kind of feisty show about using it, avoiding his gaze as she sat down.

Was she embarrassed? She looked a bit flushed, as much as Zoe could.

Tyler exhaled, realizing that his pulse was still going crazy, thump-ed-ing, thump-ed-ing…

Waiting until she was dried off, with the towel wrapped around her, he got out of the water, too, sitting on the deck, facing the sun. His body had cooled down somewhat. As much as it could around her.

She glanced at him, then looked away. What was running through her mind?

"Last night, I came back to apologize to you, but you were with Chance."

A nick of disappointment cut him. The horse hadn't wanted much to do with him last night, and all Tyler had longed to do was help the animal, with its shy gaze, its wounded nature. But that wasn't what had gotten to him. He wouldn't have minded seeing Zoe.

Wouldn't have minded at all.

"Why didn't you just say something to me?" he asked.

"You were concentrating pretty hard on Chance. I didn't want to bother you. That's why I hunted you down this morning."

Hunted him down. It had a primal tone to it, and that fired him up all over again, his skin tingling, his belly clenching.

"Chance is just taking it slow," he said. "Can't blame him, really. When you've been burned, you stay wary."

Bundled up in the towel, she glanced at him, as if thinking that he would know about staying wary.

What the hell, he thought. Why dance around this anymore?

"You're probably going to find out about my deep, dark past anyway," he said, "what, with you being a crackerjack PR lady and all that."

"I haven't looked that far into what we have on you. I was hired to do damage control on Eli's past, not yours."

"Well, you might be interested to know that the Barrons seem to attract moral hazards. My ex-wife, Kristen, was cut from the same cloth as my dad and Aunt Laura. She also decided that she'd be justified in sleeping with another man, and that pretty much put an end to our marriage."

Zoe's jaw tightened. "Great woman."

"You don't have to be outraged for my sake." He didn't stop to think that she might be surprised that he was spelling this out for her...or that *he* was just as taken aback by the honesty. "What's past is past."

He paused, then said, "I was just as livid with her as I am with my dad right now. But Kristen truly believed she was in the right. In her mind, I was also having an extramarital affair—with my job. Too much of a workaholic, too many hours spent at the office...and she deserved much more." His smile was rueful. "She was right about that part."

"What do you mean?"

"I wasn't there as much as I should've been. And when she told me that there was no way in hell that I'd ever make a good father—I would only ignore my kids—I believed that, too, maybe because I hadn't been making the time to pursue a family with her."

Zoe's gaze burned. "Sometimes, when people tell you things over and over again, you start believing them. That doesn't mean they're true."

From the passionate look on her face, he wondered if there was more to what she said. How many times had she heard that she was lower class while she lived on this ranch? How long had it taken before she'd come to believe it before her mom had spirited her away to learn otherwise?

"You're right," he said. "But Kristen kept saying that all she wanted was to be happy, and around me, she wasn't." He wiped the water from his face. "Neither of us fully realized what we were in for when we first got married. I truly thought I could do it all—work, be a family man, a good husband…"

Zoe's gaze was soft. "And Tyler Barron never fails."

Her words were like a punch. The truth hurt. Everyone had expected he would shine, and he'd expected that much out of himself, too. When he'd fallen short, he'd headed for the office, working harder, longer, losing himself there until it had spit him right back out.

Still, there were times Kristen's accusations would echo in the back of his mind. *You don't have it in you to devote yourself to anything but that company…*

As Zoe said, if you were told enough times that you were one way, it was hard to believe something else.

"So what happened in the end?" Zoe asked quietly.

He shrugged, as if it didn't matter. "Kristen took off with her lover, but they broke up pretty soon afterward. She never tried to come back to our marriage, though."

"Good riddance."

She almost sounded as if she would take up his side and come out swinging at Kristen if his ex-wife ever did try to return. That did something to Tyler, mostly in the center of him, where he'd felt half-dead for a while now.

Zoe leaned toward him, and warmth radiated out in his chest, as if it had resurrected a real heart in him.

"You know what?" she said, touching his arm. "You can forget all about that stuff now. As you said, maybe you can get to the point where what's past is past. I'd like to believe that, too."

And, for the first time in years, Tyler really did think he could put everything behind him.

Chapter Five

This time, Zoe *knew* Tyler was going to kiss her.

Or maybe she was going to kiss *him,* even though it was a million kinds of wrong, even after what she'd just said to him. He was everything she'd grown up despising—privileged and touched by gold while she'd needed to work so hard for everything she had.

And he was the son of the man she'd been hired to prop up in the media, off-limits professionally.

But none of that mattered while his deep green gaze searched her own, as if looking for an answer there—a yes, a no...

Yes, she thought, and she leaned a little closer.

Closer.

A breath away—and the nearer she came to the warmth of his skin, his mouth, the faster her mind worked.

Tyler Barron...

So *not a good idea*...

But that didn't matter as he raised his hand, resting it on the back of her neck.

Her skin flared, as if it had come alive, and the sensation echoed throughout her body—cells turning over, one by one, like a giant inner storm that tumbled downward, crashing in her belly then sighing even lower.

It had been a long time since she'd been with a man, and her nerve endings were on fire, anxiety mixed with anticipation.

Desire.

When he gently pulled her to him, she hitched in a small breath, feeling the tingle of his lips before she even touched his mouth. Then she closed her eyes, waiting to feel him, reviving a hope that had never, ever died since she'd left the ranch.

He brushed his lips over hers, softly, barely, so that a surge of longing welled up in her chest.

She reveled in the aftertingle on her mouth for a second, thinking of the innocence of a first kiss, the one she'd dreamed about with Tyler years and years ago.

But a tingle wasn't enough, and she leaned in for more, skimming her lips along his, as if testing whether or not this was for real.

He smelled like lime, as if he'd shaved with that sort of cream this morning, and she paused to savor him, then pressed her lips to his yet again.

The backs of her eyelids seemed to warm up, and she saw the color of gold.

Gold—because now that she'd bothered to get to know more of Tyler, that was what he seemed to be, and Zoe only wanted to tell him that. To show him. He might be worth tons of gold, even if his ex-wife had insisted differently.

That gold seemed to expand in her vision, warming even more, filling her. Then, as this kiss lingered, the gold exploded, breaking into a thousand different colors, every one of them flying at her, drilling into her so that trickles of arousal weakened her.

She pressed against him, bracing her hands on his bare shoulders. His skin—so smooth over all his toned muscle. She'd been trying not to look at him in those swimming shorts, had been trying to avoid checking out the breadth of those shoulders, the ridges and bumps of his stomach, his arms…

Now she felt like he was all hers, just for a minute.

Just for a kiss.

Her heart felt as if it was pumping a mile a second, about to explode, too, and she pulled away from him, just so she could get a little bit of her breath back.

She inhaled enough air into her constricted chest to clear her head, bringing her back to the moment—the birds chirping, the water lapping against the deck.

The way she was leaning her forehead against his.

Maybe she was the one who pulled away first, but before she knew it, there was a space between them. A sudden bubble that felt like a canyon.

A stolen kiss between two adults who'd forgotten their responsibilities and situations in life.

She pushed her wet hair away from her face. Just as she was about to make some kind of joke about how she'd always been curious about kissing him, his smile disappeared, and he reached up, smoothing another strand of hair from her cheek.

Those chirping birds seemed to have nested in her belly, flying around, brushing her with their wings.

He coasted a thumb to the side of her mouth. "Dimples."

It took a second for the word to develop meaning in her addled brain.

He chuckled, then skimmed over the other side of her mouth. "Yesterday, I noticed that you had a dimple, and I wondered if you'd have two. And you do."

There went her stomach again—bird-flutter crazy. He'd noticed a small detail like dimples on her. *She* barely even saw them every morning when she got ready for work.

He was near enough that she could discern every detail about his face, too—the wisps of gold nestled in the green of his eyes. The smoothness of his skin where he'd obviously shaved this morning. A little cut near his strong chin.

"You've got one, too, you know," she said, touching the slight indentation in his chin. "A dimple."

He smiled, and it was so sexy that it swept her away. She'd never thought she could be so weak and strong at the same time.

They looked at each other, and it went on a beat too long, as if their impetuous moment was turning over and becoming a reality they would both have to acknowledge in a bigger way.

She leaned back, just enough so that he took his hands away from her face.

It would've been nice to kiss him again. He made her feel as if she could do everything right, that it didn't matter about how much time had passed since she'd been with any other man. Tyler felt like the first.

"Well," she finally said, taking the bull by the horns, "when I woke up this morning, I didn't expect *that* to happen."

"Why? Aren't you used to being kissed?"

The assured way he said it brought to mind the commanding billionaire, but there was a hint of the cowboy in there, too—in charge, a man of well-chosen words, hot as heck.

She pulled the towel around her a little more. It smelled as clean as Tyler did.

"Don't get me wrong—I'm used to being kissed," she said. "Probably not enough, though."

Nice. Why'd she have to go and say something like that?

Nerves. She was still a bundle of them.

Recovering, she said, "I'm just pretty lazy about dating these days."

"Work, right?"

"It doesn't leave a lot of time."

"So there's never been anyone serious? The one who got away?"

Like your ex-wife? she thought. But she chased the notion off. It was just that her first reaction was always to put her guard up.

But why? Had the whole "lower class" deal worked her over as much as seeing her parents' marriage disintegrate?

Zoe paused for a second. Come to think of it, there'd never been a time when she'd felt as if she'd finally reached the point where she was good enough for *anyone*.

"There've only been a couple of semi-significant guys," she said, trying to explain away the question.

"They seemed like they could turn into something long-term, but I guess I got bored or they got bored after a bit."

"I can't believe anyone would lose interest in you."

A stroke of heat pushed up her body.

What was he doing, saying those kinds of things?

Heck, what was *she* doing still sitting here?

Whatever they were doing, he was at it again, reaching over and drawing his knuckles over her cheek.

"Tyler…"

Yet even as she whispered it, she was rubbing her cheek against his hand, loving the feel of his skin against her face. Thinking of what it would be like to have his palm on her waist, her stomach…*everywhere.*

When he tugged at her towel, she looked over at him, seeing the fervent need in his eyes. She had the same needs, too, and she would bet that her gaze showed him that just as clearly.

Two of a kind, she thought as the towel slumped to the deck, leaving her in that wet T-shirt.

Then he was kissing her again, harder this time, more demanding. But she was ready for that. Ready for him, even though something in the back of her mind told her to stop, because Tyler was a Barron, and she was only here to work—to stay out of his personal life so she could do her job and do it well.

Yet that was her brain talking, not her body.

Her body was saying all kinds of different things—that it was putty in his hands, that she would run her palms over him, too, shaping him however he wanted to be shaped, that he could be anything he wanted with her.

That he could be the Tyler he'd obviously lost somewhere along the way.

They kissed and kissed, slower, deeper. He brought her to him so that she was in his lap, straddling him, and as he slipped his tongue into her mouth, she answered just as eagerly, taking in everything that she'd always wanted.

It was as if something had broken out inside him, and she'd gotten him there—to a place where he knew what he wanted.

And she was a woman who knew, too.

She roamed her hands over him—his chest, his arms, his ribs and back, feeling those muscles. As she got her fill, he held her, coming up for breath from their kiss.

"Zoe," he said under his breath.

Her name, coming from *him*. She'd never thought she would hear it whispered like this, as if her name mattered. Hadn't thought to hear it from anyone.

The passion in that one word lifted her up. All her life she'd tried so hard not to feel inferior to anyone, but right now, in his arms, with him saying her name like that, there was no doubt that she was *someone*. And right now, she was his someone, and she was in a place where she'd always belonged.

He ran his fingertips along her skin, as if enthralled with the dusky color of it—a color she'd been ashamed of sometimes, because it had obviously shamed her dad. Then Tyler went lower, over her neck, to the collar of her wet T-shirt.

Lower, between her breasts.

He cupped one of them, her breath coming hard and fast. She tried to slow it down, but when he circled his thumb around an already stimulated nipple, she couldn't help gasping.

"Wet lace," he said. "Seeing you in the water, in this shirt…this bra…"

She'd guessed that he'd probably gotten an eyeful, but something wicked in her was glad about that.

"Take it off," she said.

There would be consequences for all this, but they would come later. Much later.

Now was now.

Without waiting, Tyler whisked the T-shirt off her, tossing it to the deck. Then he buried his face against her neck, kissing it, using a finger to slip into her bra cup, rubbing it over her nipple.

She groaned, pressing her head against Tyler's. His dark hair was soft against her skin. Soft and thick, just like she felt as he kept caressing her.

Then, slowly, so damn slowly, he eased off one of her bra straps, revealing her breast.

He palmed her. "You really grew up, Zoe."

She didn't know what to say. "Not that you even remember me all that well. There were a lot of us ranch rats around…"

"Zoe?"

"Yeah?"

Instead of telling her to be quiet, he pulled her down for another kiss, and she melted against him, responding to every deliberate stroke of his tongue, playing with him just as he was playing with her.

But that little resident in the back of her mind decided this would be a good time to intrude.

What's going to come afterward, huh? It's not going

to end well. You'll go your way, he'll go his, just like everyone does...

And when Tyler stopped kissing Zoe, that little voice said, *Told you so.*

But then she heard the noises from outside, off in the near distance—hooves thundering on the ground, a couple of kids whooping.

Ranch rats taking some horses out for a gallop?

Tyler rested his face against her chest, as if he couldn't believe they'd been interrupted. Or maybe relieved that they had been, because now he could get his head back together.

She just wasn't sure what he was thinking as he pushed her bra strap back up, then grabbed her shirt so she could put it back on. When she'd finished, he gave her the towel, bringing it around her again so no one would see her bra through her shirt.

His gesture touched her. Even after what'd just happened, he was a gentleman.

As if wanting to avoid any kind of label, he sent her an unreadable gaze and rolled off the deck, into the water.

Zoe stood. It was almost as if nothing had just gone on.

But that was a good thing. Wasn't it?

When he came up, he did that guy thing where he flipped the wet hair out of his eyes with one jerk of his head. Zoe's chest contracted, making it hard to breathe all over again.

"Better than a cold shower," he said, pushing back through the water away from her.

He didn't have to explain any further as she waited, wrapped in that towel. Still wrapped up in him, too.

Once in the shallows, he stood, the water dripping down that powerful chest of his. What she'd give to be crushed against it again…

No. She'd been saved from going too far, ruining all her good work and maybe even sacrificing her dignity, too. She wouldn't do it again.

"I'll see you later," she said, sounding formal, back to the PR woman. Safer. Better.

"Yeah," he said, "I suppose you will."

Before she could translate his expression, he dipped back under the water, swimming away.

She didn't know whether or not *he* meant business or…something else.

Another tingle suffused her as she left with his towel still around her, his scent filling her until she shut it out.

Tyler spent the day trying to figure out just what had gone on with Zoe this morning—what it had all meant and what he was going to do about it now.

He'd liked kissing her. But *liked* was understating it. He'd wanted to take off that bra, those cutoff jeans. He'd wanted to be inside her.

And that was when he'd decided getting back in the water would be the smartest move he could make.

A sabbatical here on the ranch was supposed to put him back together, not further scatter him, and that was what Zoe did to him—made him feel more confused than ever.

Luckily, there were things that could save Tyler from complete bewilderment. His horse rescue was one, and Tyler had spent the rest of the morning with Chance, managing to get just a little closer to him in the pasture.

Uncle Abe was another, and Tyler had taken him for a slow walk outside, having lunch and dinner with him, too.

By the time the sun had headed for the horizon, he was back on track.

For the most part.

During the walk with his uncle, they'd seen Zoe's coworkers filming around the property, and Abe had made a comment about Zoe and her job, as if to draw Tyler out in some kind of conversation about it. But Tyler had sidestepped any heavy discussion, because last night's confessions from Abe had been quite enough.

"Hmm," Abe had said regarding his nephew's silence.

Tyler knew a bad "hmm" when he heard one. "What?"

"Nothing. It's only that you're quick to leap to another topic."

"I don't want to tax you with the PR stuff, Abe."

"I'm talking more than PR. That's a pretty girl who's in charge."

"Abe…"

"What, a man can't notice?"

Tyler didn't say a word. Last thing he needed was to talk about Zoe.

After dinner, which they took in the sunroom, Tyler escorted Abe back to his quarters and then stopped by the kitchens on his way out. Mrs. Nissan usually had chocolate-chip cookies on hand, and Tyler was notorious for stealing them when he was on the premises.

He even took a few more than usual, stowing them in a napkin before making a clean getaway.

Since he couldn't avoid Zoe forever, he'd decided to

just drop by with some cookies, casually, as if he did this all the time for guests. But as he approached her cottage, he knew it was only an excuse. This thing with Zoe was gnawing away at him, and it would be a good idea to get the air cleared again, just as they'd managed to do this morning. The easier it was between them, the quicker she'd get her work done, and the sooner she would leave.

That was all.

None of her coworkers' vehicles were parked in her driveway, so he figured she was done with work for the day. He knocked on her back door, then went to the bottom of the stoop, as if not wanting to risk being too close when she opened up.

Good thing he did that, too, because, when she answered, he felt as if Chance had kicked him right in the chest.

She was dressed in fancy, strappy, red leather sandals, faded jeans and one of those eyelet blouses she might've worn back when she was a ranch kid. Except now, she filled it out very…nicely. Yeah, that was the word he was looking for. She also had her hair in a low ponytail again, exposing that soft neck he'd kissed only this morning.

"Hi," she said, and right away he could tell that she wasn't sure just how to greet him. Even so, there was something about her…

Was it his imagination or did her skin have a glow to it, as if she was happy to see him?

"Hi." He grinned, coming up one step and offering the cookie-filled napkin to her. "Mrs. Nissan had some treats out, so I came by to drop some off."

She looked puzzled for a moment, as if thinking, *Treats? Seriously?*

But then she smiled, coming out and closing the door behind her. "Treats are good. Thank you."

Damn, why did this feel like a first date?

Maybe because he couldn't forget how high she'd taken him during those kisses...

Just thinking about touching her, feeling her skin under his hands, made his jeans a little tighter.

Without thinking it through, he gestured to the stoop, which was framed by the cottage's window-boxed flowers, lace-etched shutters and rosebushes. The scent of the petals rode the air as Zoe took a seat on the step just above him. He took off his cowboy hat, lowered himself to the stairs, too, just to where he had to look up slightly to see her.

As the pink-orange of dusk flirted with the sky, he took in all of her—the shine of her hair, the long lashes that framed her stunning blue-gray eyes, the delicate cheekbones that had felt so good under his fingertips.

She peeled back the napkin, took out a cookie, then offered one to him, too. He took it, careful to avoid her skin.

If she noticed, she didn't show it. "I'm used to business dinners at this hour, not cookies."

When he didn't respond right away, she went on, as if struck by nerves. "I wanted to look good in front of clients, so I even took some wine classes. But I'll tell you something—there are times when I wish I could have ordered a good beer during those dinners instead. Or eaten cookies for dessert instead of crème brûlé."

He raised his brow. "They've got beer in the kitchens if you..."

"No, I wasn't hinting that I wanted a beer." She still hadn't eaten the cookie. "Actually, I have no idea what I'm saying."

He hadn't touched his cookie, either.

Good God, if his business associates could only see him now, tongue-tied and sitting here with a cookie in hand. Hell, he'd laugh at himself, too, if there wasn't a risk that Zoe would take it the wrong way.

But what should he tell her? *Sorry for going so far this morning, even if I wanted it to go further? I had a real good time, Zoe—now can we go back to being PR rep and unwilling client?*

"Listen," she said, using that tone he'd come to realize was her to-the-point signature. "I'm not expecting anything out of this morning. We were curious, and it just…happened."

He glanced at the setting sun. She had a measured quality to her voice. She was feeling him out, waiting to see if he contradicted the "curious/it just happened" interpretation.

Dammit, all he knew was that it'd felt good being with Zoe, that he hadn't felt so free and happy in…

Maybe not ever, but definitely since he'd been young and in love for the first time.

Yet he couldn't stop thinking that, once Zoe's work was done, she would leave. He would move on, too. And he didn't know if he had it in him to deal with another situation in which he needed to leave something behind, just as he had by giving over his life to the one Eli had engineered. It made him tired even thinking about it.

"Right," he finally said. "We were curious."

At her silence, he glanced at her. She was expressionless as she played with her napkin.

"This is the thing, though," he said. "I don't want us walking around here on eggshells. That's not productive for either of us, so I decided to make sure we were good with each other."

She raised her head, as if his confession had hit her square in the heart. Maybe it was because he'd said it so sincerely.

"I overstepped my bounds this morning, as you said," he added.

"The laughin' place got the better of you." She sent a close-lipped smile at him before she adopted a bright tone and added, "Well, it did with me, too, so there's nothing to worry about."

Why did her smile seem less than natural? And why did she seem *too* relieved that they'd gotten this off their chests…?

Then she inhaled, as if she wanted to add more.

He found himself holding his breath.

But she didn't say anything else. Instead, she broke off a part of the cookie, then nibbled at it.

Disappointment hit him. What had she wanted to tell him?

He would probably never know. He'd found out that nothing was straightforward in this world, not even Zoe. Everything had some hidden facet to it, and that was how a person got screwed. It was just that she'd seemed…different.

"We're still good," Zoe said. "I can get my work done around you on the ranch, and before we both know it, that'll be that."

And there it was.

They ate their cookies as the sun dipped below the

horizon. But even long after he went back to his cabin for the night, he could still feel her on his skin, as if Zoe might just be the one person who would never go away.

Chapter Six

The next afternoon, Zoe took a break from work and went to the stables, where she'd heard Tyler was working.

She had something to show him. No, scratch that. She was actually wondering if she could get his blessing on something so that he might cooperate in giving a few media interviews or working with her. She still hadn't given up hope that she might be able to recruit him if she played her cards right.

When she did find him, she didn't announce herself right away. She just stood at the entrance, watching as he pitched hay into a stall. He was wearing nothing but jeans and boots, just as God intended when He created Texas man and, with every jab of the pitchfork then toss of the hay, his muscles bunched under sweaty skin, his abs tightening into ridges.

She'd been pressed against that bare chest and

stomach yesterday morning. But last night, there'd been no embraces. They'd only chatted on her stoop, forging this odd truce that seemed to exist between them.

But even as his mere presence had set the butterflies loose in Zoe's stomach, it hadn't been anything like yesterday morning.

Or now.

Clutching her laptop computer against her side, she used her other hand to flap the front of another sleeveless linen blouse, getting some air in there to fight the summer sweat prickling her skin.

Correction, she thought, stopping all the fidgeting. The heat was coming more from inside than out.

Tyler finished his task and went to the bale stack, working another bunch out, then freeing it from its bindings. But before digging into it, he took out a red bandanna from his back pocket, swiped the hankie over his face and reached for a bottle of water, taking a swig.

Then, exacerbating Zoe's already helpless state, he splashed some water over his skin, glancing around the stables, taking it all in as if he loved being here.

Running the bandanna over his chest, he cleared off the water, and Zoe's brain seemed to fill with static, like a TV that had lost contact with central control.

Oh, to be that scrap of cloth...

But even though they'd had a moment yesterday, she knew that they would be inviting a whole lot of complications if she initiated something here and now, and it wasn't just because of her PR assignment, either. Neither of them were exactly pinups for exemplary relationships—he still carried baggage from that divorce of his, and she was just as skittish because of what she'd seen her own parents go through.

Just as Tyler was stuffing the bandanna back in his pocket, Zoe walked toward him, not wanting to spook him.

"Afternoon," she said, putting on a smile. She'd be damned if she would show him how much of a strain it was not to look at that chest, those arms.

He paused, obviously surprised to see her here—a businesswoman in the stables. Then a smile broke out over his face, and it just about took him over. The force of it even stopped Zoe in her tracks, a few feet away from him, and the oxygen snagged in her chest, especially when he ran a gaze from her toes upward.

He covered her legs, which were encased in a svelte pair of olive pants. He swept over her hips, her waist, her chest…finally arriving at her face.

As if sensing something in the air, a gray Arabian horse in the nearest stall nickered.

Tyler seemed to realize what he'd been doing, and he rested the pitchfork against a wall, his smile tamed. The sweet scent of hay and clover surrounded them, making Zoe a little dizzy.

She got over it—and quick. "Are you getting Chance's stall ready for him?"

"Yup, and he can move in whenever he decides it's time."

Tyler motioned toward a rear stall, away from the other horses. The Barron family used the animals for recreation, so they didn't have a huge operation going. Nonetheless, the stables were roomy enough to handle several cutting and show horses for some of the ranch rats, too.

"Don't tell me you're done with your job for the day and you've come to saddle up," he said.

Didn't she wish. She was just about dying to take a horse out.

Zoe held up the laptop. "No, I thought you might want to see something we've been working on. We're going to start to air this Barron Group commercial as soon as possible, before we go public with the family's news."

Right away, Tyler's posture went as taut as a stretched rope. She wished she wasn't the one who pulled him to such lengths, but this was her job.

"You don't have to look at the ad if you don't want to," she said, praying that he *would* come around.

A moment passed between them.

"I guess I can look at it." He walked back toward the stacked hay bales, fetching his shirt from a pile and putting it on.

Disappointed at his cool attitude—or maybe it was because he was wearing that shirt again—she followed him to the hay, set the computer on a stack, opened it up and turned it on.

Damn her for being so affected by his skin. "We figured we'd tweak an existing commercial by focusing more on the positives."

"Are you talking about the 'From our family to yours' advertisement that's been running for a year already?"

"Yes."

From our family to yours. It had been a slogan emphasizing just how giving and charitable The Group had been during tough economic times, appealing to their conservative base most of all. The former point man on the PR campaign had left Walker & Associates, and Zoe had anticipated using the ad from the day she'd been assigned to the account.

She accessed the file, but instead of keeping her eye on the commercial, she gauged Tyler instead.

The new images of meadows and horses twined with a montage of old commercial footage featuring The Group's charitable efforts—subtle flashes of the Barron Foundation's annual juvenile diabetes fundraiser and its efforts to aid down-on-their-luck local families. But now the commercial ended with archived footage from better days—Eli Barron at the diabetes event, surrounded by children and wearing a genuine smile.

As Zoe clicked off the file, Tyler remained stone-faced. She glanced at the ground, because she didn't feel all that wild about the ad, either—the insinuation that Eli was a great guy and no one should be too quick to speak badly about him.

But to be successful, she had to make her peace with this.

"No one's saying he's a saint," she said. "But your father *has* done one or two things in his life that made him a decent guy. From what I hear, he really does love to help those kids."

Tyler had crossed his arms over his chest, but when he sighed, he wasn't as stiff as usual. It was if he was trying with all of his might not to be angry.

Was he coming around in some way, day by day? *Had* this sabbatical done him some good?

"You certainly laid the groundwork for what's to come," Tyler said.

A backhanded compliment. But at least Zoe's boss had been happy about this idea of hers. And her team had been congratulatory, too.

So why didn't this minor coup feel as triumphant as she'd expected? Would the surge of happiness finally hit her when she got off this ranch and back to real life, away from Tyler?

Now that she had him in a halfway receptive mood, she went ahead with the rest.

"I've got a conference call with my team in a couple of hours, before everyone descends on the guesthouse here."

"That's where your war room is going to be?"

"During the most frantic moments of the news bomb. And, if possible, we'd like the family to be nearby, too. We're hoping everyone will agree to come here to the country while the news cycle is hopping."

"United we stand."

"That's the notion."

"Good luck then."

She ignored his cynicism. "Jeremiah's stopping by the ranch to see Abe later this afternoon, and I'll be showing him the commercial at that time, too. I could've just sent him the file on the computer, but I want to be there when he sees it." She hesitated, then came out with the worst part. "I'll be doing the same with Chet, once he arrives here later today."

Eli wouldn't be participating in the media events at first, since the board had wanted him to lie low for a while. He'd been too temperamental lately, too much of a loose cannon.

She'd expected Tyler to react, but he didn't. "When I saw Abe this morning, he was excited about seeing him."

He sounded pretty mellow about this, but Zoe bet that he was just hiding his true feelings—an inner ruckus.

Without thinking it through, she touched his sleeve. He closed his eyes, clearly holding something back. She longed to see just what was in his gaze.

When he opened his eyes, she thought she did spot a flash of emotion, although she couldn't say exactly what it was. Or if it was even about how her hand still rested on him.

Her first instinct was to back away from this man who was tossed so many different ways that she feared she could never have any of him, even if he offered it. But she held on, too stubborn or stupid to let go.

"I suppose," she said, "you'd rather stay away from the big house while Chet's visiting?"

"No. I'm going to say hi, then give him space. I think we both still need it."

True. From what Tyler had already told her, it wasn't as if Chet had been calling to discuss matters with either him or Jeremiah.

Two of a kind, him and Chet, she thought. Just like brothers, whether Tyler knew it yet or not.

She smiled up at him, hoping he would see how she admired his restraint and ability to cope when it came to the rest of his family.

"There are men who'd make this situation worse by storming up to Chet and taking their anger out on the wrong person," she said.

"It's not his fault."

But that didn't mean Tyler was accepting his new brother easily, Zoe thought. It was bad enough that every time he looked at Chet, he was going to see his dad in him. It would take a while to get over that in itself.

Tyler moved his hand so that her own slid down to his wrist, her fingertips nesting in his palm. He looked down at the sight as if just the slightest touch from her was an anchor of sorts.

Her chest warmed. Being an anchor didn't weigh her down; it felt surprisingly nice.

Really nice.

His voice was strained. "When you came back to Florence Ranch, I wanted nothing to do with you, at least after I recognized you and realized why you were really here."

She blinked. "What are you saying, Tyler?"

He paused, then shook his head.

"You're warming up to this campaign?" she asked bluntly, taking a chance.

"I wouldn't say that."

She swallowed, and she didn't know why it was so hard. Why was it so important for him to accept her? It shouldn't matter, but dammit all, it had started to.

He let go of her, gazed into her eyes. Her knees went wobbly. He had that kissing look on his face again, but it was different now. There was a gentleness in the green of his irises, a quality that simultaneously scared her and made her so happy.

Did he even know it was there?

In the background, there was a stir, making her think that someone had come into the stables.

Tyler planted his hands on his hips as he looked toward the entrance. But when the sound came again, Zoe realized that it was only a horse moving around in its stall.

She went red-hot, and not in a good way. Mortification. He'd let go of her pretty quickly. Was it because she was the daughter of the former foreman?

Was he, a Barron, still too good for her, even after she'd elevated herself?

She headed for her laptop. "Time for me to get back."

Great, her voice sounded as if it'd been torched.

"Zoe…"

He was frowning, as if he didn't understand her abruptness.

But she wasn't about to feel second-class—not ever again. Best to stop playing with fire. Best to just get out of here.

"What are you doing now?" he asked.

"Why? Do you need some help pitching hay?"

He grinned. "I'd never turn down the offer."

"Well, I'm working."

"And tonight?"

"Working."

Did he want to sit on her stoop and revel in the almost unbearable tension some more?

"Because," he continued, "I thought you might want to take a ride while you're here."

Her heart gave a leap. A horse ride, a walk in the meadow, the opportunity to run around like the ranch kid she'd once been… She wanted it all.

And it would be nice to have him doing it with her, although she knew there was no chance of that.

"Maybe some evening I'll do that," she said, already walking out of the stables.

Not even looking back to see if he *would* suggest going with her.

As always, going to Chance gave a lift to Tyler's day, just as riding and communing with horses used to do before life had become all school uniforms and business suits.

Tyler waited outside the fence, not wanting to scare the horse. After a while, he was able to make his slow way over the barrier, squatting on the grass opposite Chance, who was grazing about twenty feet off.

One minute, Tyler moved a foot closer. Then another minute, another foot.

And another.

Another.

It seemed like eons later, but Tyler ultimately got to the point where he was close enough so that Chance raised his head, acknowledging him.

Tyler didn't move except to offer his hand, just as he'd been doing ever since they'd met.

This time, though, the animal approached, nuzzling Tyler's fingers, his arm, nosing him so enthusiastically that Tyler just about lost his balance.

He laughed. It was so simple to do around Chance, but not so much with anyone else. Except...

Tyler put the image of him and Zoe at the swimming hole out of his mind.

"There, boy," he said softly. "You finally used to what's around you now?"

He kept talking as he began to stand, keeping eye contact. Chance didn't even shy away.

"You're sure looking better, even after a couple of days, aren't you?"

It was true—Chance's weight seemed to be going up instead of down, even in barely noticeable terms. And the horse seemed livelier, his eyes shining instead of looking at the world with a dull sheen. The vet would be visiting again for a checkup, and Tyler knew the report would be a positive one.

Chance had cocked one of his legs, taking the weight off it, relaxing, so Tyler laid his hand on his neck.

They stood like that for a while, until Tyler slid his palm back, gently patting his horse, bonding with him.

Eventually, Chance wandered away, toward the pasture shelter. The afternoon was easing into dusk, and it would be time for Tyler to go soon, so he saw to Chance's feed, checking over the shelter, too, until he walked to his cabin for a shower and dinner. He wouldn't rush Chance, but he couldn't wait to take him for a ride.

As he made his way down the graveled path, he thought of sitting on a stoop again tonight with Zoe, maybe even mentioning his progress with Chance to her since she'd met the horse and might be interested.

He slowed his steps. Zoe. She'd been the first to come to his mind.

But why should that rattle him when she seemed to be the only person he could really talk to right now? Jeremiah had been a decent confidant before, but Tyler had never chatted about things like Kristen or true heartbreak with him.

What was it about Zoe that made the talking simpler?

Tyler was still trying to figure it out when he passed Miguel's cabin on the way to his own.

Zoe's father was tossing some horseshoes at a stake, all by himself. When he threw the last one, the older man slowly made his way over to retrieve them.

"Tough competition?" he asked Miguel.

He squatted, picking up the horseshoes. "Keith is supposed to come over for a match and dinner after he gets his work done. I'm just warming up."

Dinner. Would Zoe be coming down here, too, cooking for the men? Or was she really working late?

Tyler didn't cotton to the notion of affable Keith standing at the grill with Zoe again. Not that there'd been any outrageous flirting going on during their dinner the other night, but...

Ah, why was he even mulling this over?

Miguel made as if to give Tyler the horseshoes, as if it was a foregone conclusion that he was here to play. Tyler insisted that the older man go first.

Miguel missed every shot. "There are some things that don't improve with age. My aim is one of them."

"I'll bet there are other things you can brag about. I heard you're pretty good at constructing model planes."

"I fly some of them, too, by remote control." The man stepped aside for Tyler to take his turn. "This is what retirement consists of—model planes, throwing horseshoes at stakes, going down to the creek for the occasional fishing session. Something for you to look forward to."

The crickets started their nightly song, and Tyler thought that if this sabbatical was anything like retirement, he could definitely live with it.

He felt loose as he threw a horseshoe, and it caught the stake, spinning around it.

"Are you some kind of champion at this?" Miguel asked.

"Pure luck."

They played a few rounds, and no matter how much

Tyler tried to lose, Miguel always managed to score lower.

Maybe Tyler's luck *had* changed for the better, beginning with the night he'd found Chance out there at the fair.

Or was it when Zoe had shown up?

Miguel rubbed his throwing arm as Tyler took another turn. The older man didn't exactly seem pained as much as he seemed worn-out.

Used, Tyler thought. Had his family used Miguel so badly over the years?

And just think—one of the things they'd given him in return was a bad marriage and maybe even a swipe to the ego that had haunted the man.

It just wasn't right that Miguel had been on the receiving end of that.

"Miguel," he said, weighing the horseshoe in hand. "There's been something I've been wanting to say to you."

"Is it about my daughter?"

Tyler practically dropped the horseshoe.

"Just joshin'." Miguel slapped his leg and chuckled as he sat on a bench. "You two have been hanging around because of her work, and I couldn't resist a poke at you. You just don't seem as imposing without your business suit, and it's easy to forget who you are."

Tyler frowned. Imposing? Was he still that way, even outside the office?

Unsettled by that, he said, "Don't give it another thought, Miguel."

The other man rested his hands on his thighs. "What'd you want to chat about?"

"I've been wanting to apologize to you for what my father said all those years ago."

Miguel crinkled his brow, as if reaching way back in his mind. The dim porch light made him look older, putting wrinkles where there weren't all that many.

"Oh," he finally said. "That."

Yeah, that.

Miguel seemed unconcerned. "It's water far under the bridge."

Not for Zoe, and Tyler suspected that it wasn't that way for Miguel, either. He was just like most men, unwilling to show how mere words could affect him. Tyler had been like that for a long time after Kristen had lit into him, too, about not being cut out to be a father or a good husband. The words had scarred over, but they were still there, a faint reminder.

"I just wanted you to know," Tyler said, "that I'm now aware of what was said, and I don't agree with my dad. None of us do, and if we could take it back, we would."

Miguel looked him in the eye now, and there was understanding in his gaze. Appreciation that he didn't even have to voice out loud for it to matter.

Tyler went back to throwing his horseshoes, wondering where he'd found the cojones to bring up the subject with Miguel. When the older man spoke, it caught Tyler off guard, since he thought Miguel had wanted to leave the subject behind.

"My only regret," he said, "is that the entire situation eventually put Zoe off the ranch. To this day, she's angrier than hell at your father."

"She told me about it." But she'd obviously contained

her own anger to the point where she didn't show it much—not the way Tyler was doing with Eli.

"She talked to you?" Miguel asked.

"Yeah."

A rush of warmth flooded Tyler, because it sounded as if Zoe didn't talk about that stuff to anyone. But she had with him.

He finished with his horseshoes. "I don't know exactly what's between you and your daughter now, but I know that she'd do anything to make up for those years you lost."

Miguel nodded, as if the words were coming hard for him. Then he finally said, "I wasn't sure for a while there, but then I got sick, and she was at my bedside in a minute flat. Part of me didn't think she'd even come."

"A woman like Zoe will always be there," Tyler said, not realizing just how true that might be until now.

Miguel sat still, as if gathering himself, then got up to take his turn. As he passed Tyler, he patted him on the arm.

The only person who'd done that to Tyler so naturally was Abe.

Just as Tyler was about to sit, he glanced at the porch, spying someone in the shadows, standing under the amber light as if they'd been there for a while.

Zoe?

His veins tangled as he recognized her in a skirt and one of those sleeveless blouses she liked. She also wore an expression that was so nakedly sorrowful that he wanted to save her from it.

He wanted to keep her from ever feeling sad again.

When she saw that she'd caught his attention, she straightened up and went into her father's cabin.

Tyler glanced back at Miguel, who'd actually hit the stake this time.

"I'll be back," he said.

"Take your time, Terminator. I'm on a roll."

Tyler entered the cabin to find Zoe taking a plastic bag of fresh spinach out of the refrigerator.

"You heard?" he asked.

"I heard."

She closed the door, and he steeled himself for a scolding about how he'd stuck his nose where it didn't belong. But he would take it, mostly because he was *glad* he'd crossed a personal line.

All part of clearing the air, he thought. All part of that path to forgiveness he was heading toward.

When she turned to him, she was smiling a small smile. "Thanks for saying all that out there."

Now he smiled, too. In fact, he felt like kicking his boot at the braided rug on the ground, but he fended off the aw-shucks moment.

Instead, he came closer to her, unable to stay away. She looked up at him, questions riddling her storm-blue eyes, as if she wouldn't know what to do if he touched her again, as he'd done in the stables this afternoon.

He didn't know what he would do, either, to tell the truth, and he backed away ever so slightly.

She chuffed, beginning to open the spinach bag. "That's right. Someone might come in and see you with the ranch rat."

Whoa. All he'd done was move away from her an inch because he didn't need the temptation.

"Are you saying that you think I don't want anyone seeing me close to you?" he asked.

She didn't answer.

Good God, it had never even crossed his mind. He'd remembered a few vague things about Zoe Velez from the past, and none of them had been about her "lower" status on this ranch. And all he saw now was a determined, vibrant woman who had the world at her feet.

"You're wrong about that," he said, feeling impulsive in the face of her accusation. He wasn't "that man" anymore—Eli's puppet son. "Would you think the same way if I brought you up to the big house to meet with Abe over dinner? I know you've talked briefly with him on the phone on good days because of the PR stuff, but he's been asking about the campaign."

Damn—that had come out the wrong way, and as she sent him a told-you-so look, he corrected himself.

"I want you to meet him in a personal setting. Tomorrow, if you can."

Just like that, her expression gentled. Did she know what Abe meant to him?

It occurred to Tyler that what he'd just done was pretty huge—suggesting that he introduce her to the man who'd meant even more to him than his own father.

But it was too late to take it back, even though Tyler's panic button had been pushed.

"Dining with Abe would be great," Zoe said.

She paused, then offered him the spinach, silently asking him to wash it, a full smile turning up the corners of her lush mouth.

He took the spinach from her, and even through the panic, that glow made its way to the center of Tyler, where his heart beat faster, anticipating tomorrow.

Chapter Seven

"So you invited a girl for dinner," Jeremiah said, pausing over the pool table in the mansion's lounge, cue stick poised to knock in the eight ball.

Tyler leaned back against the wall, drink in one hand and pool cue in the other. The way his younger brother was acting, you would think tonight was some kind of event—like Tyler was introducing the family to his high-school sweetheart.

The very idea struck him hard. He'd only invited Zoe for dinner and to meet Abe to prove he wasn't the type of guy she'd been raised to believe was a rich jerk.

"Don't make a big deal out of tonight," Tyler said.

Jeremiah chuckled, and it made his eyes go squintier than usual. He'd attempted to tame back his thick, dark blond hair, but a wave still flopped over his forehead as he took his shot at the cue ball, sending it clicking into the eight, which rolled into a pocket.

From the looks of it, anyone would think that his younger brother hadn't a care in the world. He was certainly partying enough, as if to dash away any suspicion that he was suffering under the burden of the scandal, too—that he was fighting some kind of crisis of confidence triggered by Chet's standing as the new favorite son.

Did Jeremiah, who'd always been ignored in favor of Tyler, first, and now Chet, feel more disposable than ever?

Tyler put down his drink and rested his stick against the table, then began to rack 'em up for another bout. "Zoe's a guest on the property, so why is it such a big deal if she comes up to the mansion?"

"You're right. Inviting a pretty woman to dinner is never a remarkable event—especially for you, seeing as you're in the habit of dating like a glutton, anyway."

Tyler shrugged off the jibe. "I go out."

"Yeah, to charity events and business dinners with your female associates who won't demand anything out of you beyond that night. As I said, Ty—you're a huge Romeo."

Racking the pool balls a little rougher than was necessary, Tyler ignored his brother.

Jeremiah leaned against the table, his posture lazy, clashing with the crisp lines of his Armani suit. He had shed his jacket, tossing it carelessly over the back of an antique chair nearby.

"As memory serves," he said, "Zoe was a tomboy when we were young, but she really sprouted, didn't she?"

Tyler felt some temper—or was it something else?—

creep up his skin. "Hey, she's working for the family now."

A flush, for God's sake. When the hell was the last time he'd done something like that?

Jeremiah chuckled some more, having a grand old time. "Don't worry. If you're thinking that I have romantic designs on Zoe, I don't."

"Good." Protective. Why should he sound that way when he had no reason to be? "I hear you're busy enough with half the women in San Antonio, anyway. No sense in breaking more hearts out here."

Especially Zoe's.

Jeremiah went quiet. Obviously, Tyler had hit a sore spot, and it didn't have as much to do with Zoe as with how Jeremiah had been going from woman to woman lately.

Like brother like brother, Tyler thought. Jeremiah had his women to distract him, just as Tyler had used work.

Or, at least, how he *had* always used his work. Past tense. Now there were other, more important things in life. Like…

As Tyler paused, he saw Zoe in his mind's eye, just as she'd been at the swimming hole, in those cutoff shorts and a T-shirt.

The country girl of his dreams.

But he erased the thought, putting away the rack and gesturing for Jeremiah to go first.

In response, his brother merely ran a gaze over him, taking in Tyler's cowboy boots, his faded jeans.

Then he grinned.

"What're you smiling about?" Tyler asked.

"You just seem…good. Different. That's all."

Longing wedged itself in Jeremiah's words, as if he thought Tyler had discovered something important by leaving work and coming back to the ranch.

Tyler glanced at Jeremiah's suit, expecting to find a certain yearning in himself, too.

But…hellfire.

He didn't want to be wearing a suit. The very notion even made him want to tug at his collar.

Jeremiah took a shot, breaking the triangle of balls apart, sinking a stripe, then stalking the table.

"When are you coming back to The Group?" he asked.

"I haven't set a date." Truth be told, he hadn't even been thinking much about it. "Who knows if Dad will even let me back in? He told me that if I didn't change my attitude, I wouldn't be welcome."

"Bull. You're the backbone of that company—always behind every deal, always there to stand behind the staff in their decisions. Don't let him psych you out." Jeremiah put another stripe into a pocket. "He's going to need you more than ever when this PR crap fully hits."

Tyler picked up his cocktail. "It's his mess. Let him handle it."

Jeremiah rose from his hunch at the pool table, looking at Tyler as if he were an utter and complete stranger—a denim-clad enigma who'd wandered out of the meadows and into the mansion.

"Damn," Jeremiah said. "I never thought I'd see the day."

"The day that I refused to be his minion?"

"You've always been… I don't know. *There*."

"I'm still there, Jer." And he felt there…no, *here*…

more than ever. He'd never been so present, so aware of who he was more than right now.

He'd changed.

The realization ricocheted around his head, and he tried to grab on to the train of thought underlying that realization.

So what was life about now if he'd changed? Was it about losing the urgency to work and succeed? Finding a measure of peace here in the country, away from the hustle and bustle, and falling back into what felt right?

Or was it about what Zoe had said about struggling with bitterness and finding it within himself to forgive— especially by curbing the anger he'd been directing at himself for making the wrong choices in life, for listening to someone or something else besides what was in his own heart?

Tyler's shoulders relaxed at the realization. He couldn't hate himself, as he'd been doing.

Zoe had put him in a position to see that, whether she knew it or not.

Jeremiah took another shot, missing the pocket. He walked away. He didn't like missing.

"Have you thought of how you're going to deal with Dad when he gets back from his trip?" he asked casually.

Casual. Right. "Yeah, I have."

"Same here. And when I do see him, I'm sure all my best intentions will fly right out the window. I have to say, though, that after you told me about how Uncle Abe had been pulling Dad's strings in all this, it calmed me somewhat. I was angry at Dad for announcing Chet's birthright to us while Abe was still sick, and your news put a different spin on everything."

Tyler prepared to take his turn at the table, but he was tense. Just talking about Eli made the anger rise.

Why couldn't he be like Zoe, trying harder to let go of the rancor when it came to others?

He already knew. It was because forgiveness allowed people like his father to get away with bad behavior over and over again. Forgiveness seemed like such a naive response when it came to people like Eli.

Still, how would it feel to be free of the rage that was constantly hammering at him?

He took a shot. Missed.

Tonight didn't seem to be his night.

As Jeremiah returned to the table, boot steps sounded on the floor, near the lounge door.

When Tyler turned, he saw Chet, standing at the entrance, his hands in his jeans pockets, his shoulders stiff.

Tyler glanced at Jeremiah, who'd straightened up from the table. Jeremiah was taller, leaner, like their mom, but both he and Chet had the same dark blond hair and blue eyes as Eli.

Awkward silence hung between them like a thick curtain until Tyler couldn't stand it anymore. "Good to see you," he forced himself to say to Chet. "Sorry we didn't cross paths last night when you dropped by."

Could he sound any more formal?

Jeremiah had leaned his pool cue against the table. "You up for a drink?"

It was as if that curtain had fallen smack on top of them and none of them knew how to get out from under it.

Chet held up a hand. "No, thanks. I've got to go out of town again, but before I left, I thought I'd check in with my dad."

All of them froze, because Abe wasn't Chet's dad. Not technically.

The words seemed to be twisting inside Chet, squeezing him and draining him, and he shoved his free hand back into his pocket, his shoulders hunched.

Damn our father for doing this, Tyler thought, the fury stoked and burning inside him so ferociously that he couldn't ever imagine dousing it.

But then one of the downstairs employees announced their main guest for the night.

Zoe entered the lounge like a cool breeze on fevered skin, wearing a flowered summer dress and those red strappy sandals. She was smiling, unaware of the tension between the brothers.

For a minute, her smile was Tyler's lifeline.

But then she took a glimpse around the room, and that smile faded.

"I can come back another time," she said.

"No."

Tyler didn't think he'd said anything more emphatically in his life. He wanted her here.

Wanted...*her.*

The depth of his need made his pulse stomp. He didn't even care if Jeremiah or Chet knew it.

Straightforward, honest Zoe. The only person in this room who had any chance of keeping him sane right now.

Before he went to her, he addressed Chet. "You're staying for dinner?"

Maybe they could really talk afterward, wipe some of this mangled stuff out of their way.

"I..." Chet shook his head. "I won't be able to hang around all that long. Maybe I'll make it here in a week, when I get back to San Antonio."

A rejection, showing that Chet was about as ready to put all this behind him as Tyler or Jeremiah was.

"All right," Tyler said.

As he walked to Zoe, then to the hallway with her, she looked up at him with those empathetic, blue-gray eyes and did exactly what he needed.

She touched his arm again, not saying a word. But all the same, he knew she understood.

Just as she always seemed to.

"It'll still be an hour yet before dinner," Tyler said, resting his hand on the small of Zoe's back, guiding her out of the lounge and into the foyer, with its grand staircase and crystal chandelier. "I'd planned for some cocktails, but..."

He trailed off, yet Zoe didn't even need him to say that Chet's arrival had put the kibosh on happy hour. She'd never read anyone so easily in her life, even if he did have a tendency to be so damn opaque.

Heck, the moment she'd stepped into that lounge, she'd seen right away that he'd taken a hit because Chet had returned. And she'd known right down to the bottom of her heart what Tyler needed.

To forget for a short time.

To go back to the freer-and-easier man who was trying to start over.

"How about you show me around the mansion then?"

she asked. He still had his hand on her back, and the contact was making her legs wobbly.

"You've never seen it?"

"Just a couple of times, but it's been forever. And I mostly stayed in the kitchens."

His hand fell away from her back, and Zoe cursed herself for opening her big mouth. Why did she have to bring up the reminder of their disparate places in life?

Then again, if it wasn't her job coming between them, this was always going to do the trick, wasn't it?

Zoe bolstered herself. Who cared where she'd started when she'd ended up in such a good place, anyway?

He took her into the study first, with its banks of leathered books and a wooden ladder that slid on a track along the walls. An impressive oak desk stood in front of a burgundy velvet-curtained window that overlooked the sweeping expanse of front lawn.

She wandered to the window, peering out of it. "I can see the guesthouse."

Joining her, he leaned over her shoulder, looking out, too. His chest pressed into her back, and she smelled the clean, musky scent of him, felt his warmth branding her. Her veins seemed to turn to rubber.

But she wasn't ever going to feel weak again.

"When I was little," she said, "I used to imagine living in this place. I'd picture myself going to the parties you would throw and sliding down the banisters." She laughed. "I was obsessed with the huge staircase in this house."

"I have to confess to sliding down a few rails in my time."

His words vibrated from his chest and through her

back. She swallowed, recovering, allowing the curtain to fall so that her view was blocked.

He began to move away from her, but she stopped him with her next comments.

"Just think. From the cabins to a guest cottage… Next thing you know, I'll be in a house just like this one."

She'd been kidding, but his silence spoke volumes. All she'd been doing was trying to lighten things up. If their differences didn't matter, why shouldn't they be able to joke about them?

She turned to him, ready to tell him that she hadn't meant anything by what she'd said.

But then they locked gazes, and the words got lost.

Green eyes, so deep that she could fall into them if she didn't take care…

She went to the desk, pretending that it was the most interesting item in the room.

"So what's next on the tour?" she asked, sounding superchipper.

Tyler seemed to notice her nerves, too, and he averted his face, as if to hide his smile. But hiding it only made a spark go off in her.

He exited the study, and she walked behind him.

"What's so funny?" she asked.

"Nothing."

"Is it because I'm trying to avoid stepping on those hundred thousand land mines between us?"

Her bluntness made him stop in the hallway. Slowly, he faced her, and with every passing nanosecond, her heartbeat escalated.

He had one of his eyebrows raised. "You sure don't hold much back, do you, Zoe?"

"It's just the truth. You were looking at me like…"

The eyebrow arched even more. "Like…?"

Good heavens, she'd forgotten how he'd *been* looking at her. All she could see was now.

He had that kissing look again, and she couldn't take another false start with him. When they'd agreed that they'd both just been curious at the swimming hole— that they'd shared little more than a kiss and that was all—it had nearly bruised her inside, and she wasn't about to open herself up to another punch like that.

"Let's go this way," he said, as if unable to figure the both of them out, either.

He headed down the hallway, and it was beyond her to stop herself from following, especially when she saw how his blue jeans clung so nicely to his rear.

Especially when he drew her so temptingly with those shoulders, that corded back…

God, she did love his back—how firm it had been under her hands. How strong. Worst of all, there were a lot of other parts to him that caught her fancy.

He was the whole package, she thought. The solid man she'd always believed she'd needed, the kind of guy who would hold his own against anyone if pushed, unlike what her mother had thought of her father.

When he brought her to a set of double doors, she hesitated, feeling again like that ten-year-old who'd dreamed of what was inside the big house.

"Is it…?" she asked.

He opened up the doors, revealing the ballroom.

Zoe just stood there like a dolt, staring at the marble floors and walls, the ornate golden chandeliers, the huge French doors that overlooked the gardens out back.

"You can go in," he said, sounding amused.

But the little ranch rat in Zoe couldn't follow Tyler, who'd always gone back to the big house, leaving her behind when they were young.

"Come on," he said, taking her by the hand and bringing her inside.

Before she knew it, she was in the middle of that ballroom floor, hearing music in her mind, imagining what it might be like to wear a pretty dress that swished around her legs as a man like Tyler spun her around.

Her throat burned, because there'd been so many years of dreaming, and here she was.

Or wasn't.

As she came down from the music and dreaming, she saw an empty room before her. But it was filled with Tyler in his cowboy outfit, his thumbs hooked into his belt loops.

Completely filled.

Zoe seemed to fold outward, every bit of her body losing form as she softened under his gaze. He was watching her as if he knew he'd been in her brief fantasy. And now it seemed as if he still saw her wearing a gorgeous dress, with her hair swept away from her neck and pinned with jeweled combs, her arms covered up to the elbows in satin gloves.

Zoe felt like a real princess for the first time in her life, and it was only because of one look from this man, not because she was in a ballroom or at a real dance or because she'd finally become one of them.

"I wish," he said, "that there was a reason to have a party in here right now."

The reminder of his family issues—his disappointments—made her come down a little.

"I'm not dressed for a party, anyway," she said.

"Sure you are."

He hesitated, his gaze dark until he swept another look down her body, then back up.

Then it was as if he couldn't help moving toward her, his boots thumping on the floor, echoing throughout the room. Her heartbeat wove through her skin, making all of her pound.

"I'm just in a sundress, Tyler." It was an excuse to keep him at a distance, a last-ditch effort to maintain some measure of safety, because if he got too close, it would be over.

She wouldn't be able to talk herself into staying away.

A tremble slid through her belly as he came even closer, then rested his hand on her bare shoulder, slipped it down her arm. The tremors in Zoe's belly speared outward.

"Don't be silly," she said.

"This is far from silly." He slid his hand into hers, putting his other one on her waist.

And, just like that, they were dancing to their own music.

When he swayed with her, only slightly, a song burst out in her chest, and she closed her eyes, thinking she was going to wake up any time now.

But when she opened her eyes, Tyler was still there, looking down at her in a way she'd never thought she would see.

She heard herself talking, to make light of the situation, as if she was still the ranch rat, as if they were tucked back into a faraway time that was nowhere near this scary, immediate present.

"When I was a kid, I would've given my entire 'N Sync collection to be doing this."

"With them?"

"No." She laughed, trying to sound careless. "With you."

His lips parted, but she spoke first.

"I had a bit of a crush on you back then."

She hoped he'd heard that last part loud and clear. *Back then.*

He smiled, and she just about dropped to the floor. Fortunately, he was holding her.

"That's when you were a kid, huh?"

Was he asking if she *still* had a thing for him?

What was he doing? Egging this moment on? Hadn't they come to an understanding that intimacy wasn't in the cards for them?

She swerved around the answer he'd been hinting at. "I just thought you were pretty cute. That's all."

He laughed softly, and once again, she could feel him buzzing into her.

"I wish I'd known you had a thing for me," he said.

"Why? We were ten when I left. It's not like we would've dated."

"I might've kissed you or something, during one of those hide-and-seek games. I don't remember that well, but you might've been pretty cute, too."

Desire spun through her. She'd been kissed by him over twenty years later, and her body wasn't about to stop reminding her of it.

"You should've just kissed me anyway," she said. "Or were girls yucky to you back at that age?"

He made a thoughtful face, then said, "Ten years old? Girls definitely had the cooties. I didn't make my first move with anyone until sixth grade. Hell, Jeremiah even beat me to getting a real kiss."

"If you'd just kissed me, you would've been *my* first," she said. "And I'm sure it would've been a lot better than what I ended up with."

"Really?"

"Yikes, mine was a letdown. A red-haired boy in middle school named Karl Williams. I just remember it was really awkward and I ignored him for about a week afterward."

"That's too bad. You should have good memories of a first kiss."

"But I do." *Of ours.*

That part went unsaid, but she was certain he'd understood.

They stopped swaying.

"There wasn't anything innocent about the one we had," he said.

He was right—there'd been fire and heat, an over-whelming desire to make up for what she'd never gotten from him...or anyone.

Yet now... Now he'd obviously decided to rewrite history, as he cupped a hand under her jaw, rubbing a thumb along her cheek. She stifled a moan, because she knew what was coming. Was dying for it.

She didn't think about how he would no doubt break her heart as he bent to her, touching his lips to hers so tenderly that a sadness rose up in her. Sadness because she'd missed years of this kind of connection with anyone.

And she'd had to go and fall for a man who was far more complicated and out of bounds than all the others.

As she fell even further, floating, losing every grip she'd clung to before in her life, Tyler's kiss lingered, resplendent with warmth and possibility, softness, promises of making her forget about anything or anyone but him.

It was so sweet that it took the place of that first kiss with the red-headed boy entirely.

This was the first time.

She only wondered if it would turn out to be the last as he drew away from her, still cupping her face, still looking down at her.

Biting her lip, she put some space between them. Dammit, she'd only come over here for dinner with Abe. That was what she'd told herself, anyway.

Now she and Tyler were right back where they'd started, playing this game that didn't seem to have any rules. The only outcome would be hurt. That was all that ever seemed to come out of relationships, and he should know better, too.

She turned around, leaving before he could. Once she was out of the ballroom, his boot steps trailed her as she walked down the hallway, not knowing if she should turn around to say more to him.

Or if she should just go.

But where? Back to her guesthouse?

"Zoe?" His voice was ragged.

He wanted her to stay, to "clear the air" again, no doubt. But just as she was flailing to answer him, she heard a crash of glass from the direction of the lounge.

An unsteady male laugh.

When she glanced at Tyler behind her, she knew he'd

figured out who'd also come to the big house tonight, along with everyone else.

Purposefully, Tyler strode into the lounge and, God help her, she was right behind him, backing him up.

As they entered, an older man was kicking at some broken crystal on the floor, spilled liquor pooling around the shards. He reached for another glass from the minibar, but when he sensed other people in the room, he faced them.

His gaze greeted Tyler with a spark of hazy challenge.

"And there he is," said Eli Barron, his skin ruddy, his voice slurred. "My boy, Ty, back to greet dear old Dad."

Chapter Eight

It was all Tyler could do to contain himself as he faced his father.

"Where did Jeremiah and Chet go?" he asked, his voice so gritty he thought for certain he could spit out gravel.

His dad shot a belligerent glance around the room, then held up his hands. "They told me I was drunk, and they'd rather say a decent hello when I sobered up. I don't know what was up their craws, because I was real polite when I walked in." He cocked his head at Tyler. "Luckily, you're here to welcome me now."

The sarcasm abraded him. "Sounds like you got welcome enough from all the booze in your limousine on the way over here."

His father barked out a laugh, and it wasn't until Zoe tightened her hold on Tyler's shirt that he even realized someone else was in the room.

He looked down at her, and when she glanced back, there was a steadiness in her gaze that soothed him.

Eyes the color of still water. The memory of what she'd said at the swimming hole.

I'm trying to let go of it all...the bitterness...

And, in her gaze, he saw that she believed he could rise above his father, even as Eli tried to drag him down.

Her unexpected faith lent Tyler the temporary strength to control his temper, and he made sure his voice was level. "None of us realized you were coming back tonight."

His dad fumbled with a replacement glass from the minibar. "Can't a man return to his own house without catching this kind of grief?"

Tyler felt pressure from his pulled shirt.

Zoe.

After snatching the bourbon decanter, Eli poured a sloppy dose of amber liquid into his glass. "I'd heard Chet was headed here tonight, so that's why I came, too."

When Tyler fisted his hands—his father had come back for Chet, no other reason—Zoe slid her palm to his back.

He felt his center holding, her touch infusing him, solidifying into a pillar that kept him standing tall.

You're doing great, her touch said, even when it had told him so much of the opposite when they'd been in that ballroom.

Confusion about what happened whenever he touched her. Bewilderment at the feelings she was experiencing—emotions he didn't understand in himself, either.

Then, with the most telling gesture of all, she left him alone with his father.

But even as she walked out of the room, Tyler still felt her there—the imprint of her hand on his back, the lingering smell of that shampoo she used.

Yeah, still there.

"Uncle Abe told me everything," he said. "He wanted us to understand why you'd pulled this secret out of a hat while he was still recovering."

Eli had wandered away from the minibar by now. "So you know about all Abe's plans to secure Chet his deserved place in the family and The Group?"

"Yes."

"Good." His dad waved around his drink in a kind of clumsy salutation. "Would you ever have guessed that my brother had the steel to make those sorts of demands?"

It was a rhetorical question, Tyler thought as his father stopped in front of the old portrait, staring up at the specter of his deceased wife.

The ghost of what their family used to be.

"Thank God the storm hit after Florence died," Eli said softly. "I never intended her any embarrassment."

"You might have thought of that before taking Aunt Laura to bed."

"It was only a couple of times," he said, slurring. "We knew that we were doing something wrong and we kept telling ourselves to stop. And we did. But you have to understand—Florence and I weren't exactly in the first flush of love, anyway, and I thought…"

He made another grand, inebriated gesture with his glass, then took a long drink from it.

Meanwhile, a memory rustled through Tyler. His

own ex-wife saying, *I just want to be happy. I deserve to be happy.*

Tyler's voice sounded as if it was being ripped apart. "Have you realized yet what you did to everyone else just because you were looking for a quick fix?"

His dad's shoulders shook once, and he pressed his hand over his face, his back still to Tyler.

Dammit.

The anger he'd held in such check lanced him again. His father was playing the victim. That was how he would try to gain forgiveness.

The spot where Zoe had touched Tyler on his back was burning, as if she was right by his side.

Forgiveness takes work, and I'm doing everything I can to get there, she'd said.

Couldn't he do it, too? If only for Abe's sake? Forgiveness was what would allow him to accept Chet as a brother...

When his dad didn't turn away from the picture, Tyler dug in like a man, taking his first step. The hardest one.

"Dad," he said.

Out of nowhere, his father hurled his cocktail glass against the fireplace, and it shattered into a thousand pieces.

Then he turned on Tyler. "You haven't been talking to me like a man who wants to come back to The Group." His face was as red as his eyes.

But he'd said something that stuck in Tyler.

He *wasn't* a man who wanted to go back to The Group.

A sense of freedom allowed him to hold his ground.

"You're right. I don't sound like the kind of man who needs to get back to work at all."

His father obviously saw the change in him, too, and Tyler thought he also witnessed fear in his dad—the instant when a parent realizes that he has lost control of his child.

"Ty," his father said, "you know it's just the liquor talking through me tonight. I've had a tough couple of weeks, so I overindulged on the plane and in the limo over here. You see that, right?"

"Of course. And maybe it was the liquor that put me on sabbatical, too. Maybe booze was what told me that some time off would teach me my place." He laughed roughly. "The thing is…being away from work did show me a thing or two. I think you didn't expect that to happen."

The blood in Tyler's veins was flowing with even more serenity now. He felt as if he was made of the sun-dappled water in the swimming hole, the infectious laughter he'd heard from Zoe while they splashed and enjoyed each other's company on that summer's morning.

Then he pictured Zoe in the pasture with him and Chance—saw her looking at him in a way he hadn't been able to figure out until right now.

She admired him for what he'd invested in Chance, for standing up to his dad. He hadn't earned that admiration in any office.

Tyler didn't blink under his father's narrowed gaze. Eli Barron never lost anything, whether it was a deal or a son, and he sure as hell wasn't going to let *this* go.

"You think a show of defiance against me is going to help out the family?" Eli's words had gone crisper. "I know you, Ty, and if you leave The Group under these circumstances, it'll reflect badly on the business you helped shape. That would kill you."

"There's more to life than—"

"That company is your life." His dad had brought out the big guns. "You even gave up a family with Kristen to nurse The Group."

The comment tore into Tyler like a well-aimed bullet, and it ripped open his skin, revealing the raw vulnerability beneath. All he could do was cover the wound with what came most easily.

Fury made Tyler clench his jaw.

Forgiveness?

Screw it. Bitterness was all Eli Barron would ever understand.

And maybe it was the same with him, too.

"Don't you play that card with me."

"If what I said isn't true, would it jerk your chain this much?"

The rage that he'd been suppressing blasted to the surface, and it was all Tyler could do to keep himself from slamming Eli against a wall, just as he'd almost done the night of the announcement.

Jeremiah wasn't even here to stop him this time, but as he took a step toward his dad, someone else was.

"Tyler," Zoe said from the doorway.

Just the sound of her was like a pair of arms wrapping around him, holding him back. He stared at the rug, not wanting her to see him like this.

But she didn't leave him. No, instead she came to him again, and he started to breathe.

Started to come back.

"I couldn't help hearing from outside the door," she

said. "Mr. Barron, how about taking this discussion up tomorrow between the two of you?"

His father was laughing under his breath, as if it was hilarious that a former ranch rat like Zoe Velez had the gall to suggest what was best for a Barron.

And, in that second, Tyler saw the man who'd tossed a racial slur Miguel Velez's way so very casually, never even apologizing for it. Eli Barron hadn't neglected to offer an apology because he was embarrassed about what he'd said—he'd just been above extending one.

His own father, the man he'd looked up to until his sheen had slowly but surely worn off...

Eli toasted Zoe. "Public relations at its finest. It looks like it was money well spent to have you around, even to prevent more trouble in the family. You serve us well, sweetheart."

Zoe's chin lifted a notch, but she kept her composure. Tyler's nails bit into his palms.

She spoke levelly. "Mr. Barron, I think—"

"What *do* you think?" A slash of sorrow invaded Eli Barron's voice. "Can you fix *this* mess, too?"

It was almost as if he was truly asking, that he hoped she could.

But Tyler didn't have it in him to feel sorry for the man. Not after how he'd spoken to Zoe like nothing but a servant.

Tyler moved in front of her, as if shielding her. "Don't talk to her that way."

He thought he heard her take in a breath behind him. Him, Tyler Barron, defending her against his dad, the man he'd always put above everyone else.

And it felt absolutely right.

"What way?" Eli asked.

"The way you speak to everyone. You're on the road to treating her like you treated her father."

At first, Tyler thought Eli completely understood, that he recalled the day he'd made that awful slur against his former foreman. His gaze even held an apology, and, briefly, Tyler could actually imagine forgiving him. Remorse would open the door.

But in the next instant, a cocky grin settled over his face.

"Maybe us Barrons are beyond fixing," Eli said. "And maybe this is too big of a job for a little second-rate ranch rat to handle, anyway."

Zoe flinched.

"Enough," Tyler said.

His father's face went blank, as if he was fully aware he'd overstepped but didn't want to admit it.

Tyler wasn't holding back now. "You hurt Zoe and her family *once,* but no more. Never again."

"When was the first time?" his dad asked.

"Good God, you really have no idea?" Tyler said.

Zoe had crossed her arms over her chest, and the sight of this vibrant woman staying so quiet, maybe even feeling like the ranch rat she'd tried so hard to leave behind, drove Tyler to the brink.

"I..." his dad said.

"You don't remember what you said to Miguel Velez?"

His father pressed his lips together. He *did* remember. And he was too proud to admit that, too.

"You make me sick," Tyler said, holding his hand out for Zoe to take.

As she accepted his offer, her heart was in her eyes,

beating there with pulses of color and an emotion so deep that Tyler couldn't name it.

When she burrowed her hand into his, he started to lead her out of the lounge.

But Eli wasn't done.

"Ah, I get it." He laughed. "You and the ranch rat, huh? Tyler, I expected better."

It was a sad attempt to get Tyler to lose it completely, but he was beyond even rage now, and he kept walking out the door with Zoe.

"Go to hell, Tyler," his dad said.

That should've destroyed him, just like it would any "good" son. But Tyler only shook his head.

"Obviously, you've already cornered hell, Dad," he said, continuing out the door with Zoe.

But she dug her heels in, as if not wanting to leave just yet.

"Mr. Barron," she said, her voice starting out soft. Then it got stronger. "*Eli.* I can't tell you how long I admired the Barrons. I wanted to be just like you. But now..."

She returned to the plainspoken, proud woman Tyler had grown so used to—the determined fireball who overcame all her obstacles.

"Now," she said, "your opinion isn't worth the breath you had to sacrifice to speak it."

Tyler put his arm around her and got her out of there before his dad exploded.

But when he looked back at him, he was shocked to see only a man who'd been devoured by the same type of shame Miguel Velez had probably felt, too.

* * *

Zoe's heartbeat raced as she and Tyler made their way to her guesthouse.

Who was that girl who had talked back to Eli Barron?

Her—that was who. And she and Tyler had given him a taste of reality together, like a team.

The rough feel of his hand over hers flinted against Zoe's senses, creating more sparks.

A team. A pair who'd stood up for each other. *Them.*

She caught a ride on that euphoria most of the way to the guesthouse, until her own reality set in.

"Great," she said.

"What?"

"I just got myself fired, didn't I?"

"You're not going anywhere."

"Don't be cavalier." The weight that had been pressing down on Tyler seemed to have transferred over to her now, resting on her chest like a punishing, flat stone. All her hopes, her dreams, gone, just like that. "I lit into the man who hired my firm to do business with him."

Outside her guesthouse, the glow from the porch light complemented the hushed colors from the falling sun. Both caressed Tyler's cheekbones, the dimple in his chin…the slight smile on his face.

"You were amazing, Zoe." He wound his fingers through hers. "Maybe you don't realize it, but you came to my rescue in there. If you hadn't interrupted, I might've really done some damage to that man."

"I heard what was going on outside the door. I wanted to stick around in case things spun out of control." She put her free hand over her face. "Did you catch what I said, though? I'm dust."

"No. You're not." He grasped both her hands in his, taking them away from her face. "The board won't stand for my dad to fire you right now—they're the ones who actually hired Walker & Associates. And Jeremiah and I will fight to the death to keep you on."

"You…" She shook her head, as if she hadn't heard him right. "*You* would do that for me?"

He nodded, and she knew he'd turned a corner to a place that left just the two of them together.

A team.

A second pounded by, and it seemed like the next second never even came along at all. She was pinned to Tyler, trying to understand what had just happened.

He apparently caught on to the significance of his comments, how they'd bowled over Zoe, because he grasped her hands almost too tightly, as if he was just as confused about what it all meant as she was.

She held on, only because she didn't want him—the man who'd been wounded so many times before—to change his mind.

"The reason I had courage enough to talk back to your father," she said, "is that…" Her throat had heated, but she tried to talk past it. "Tyler, around you, it's easy to believe that I'm big enough to face anyone, even a powerful, intimidating man like your dad."

He released her hands, planted his palms on his hips, as if girding himself against her straight-to-the-gut words.

"Don't," she said. "Don't shut me out." They were beyond that now. They had to be.

As if he was more baffled than ever, he sauntered

toward her door. In the background, a car meandered down the long driveway. She could hear the purr of its engine.

Tyler looked toward the sound, too, and he didn't have to say that it was probably his dad being driven off the premises, retreating to his town house in the city until he could sober up and face his sons the right way.

Tyler's cell phone rang, and he answered it. Zoe tried not to eavesdrop, but all he was saying were a bunch of *Mmm-hmm*s and a final, "We'll take a rain check then."

He put the phone back in his pocket. "That was Abe's nurse. He said my uncle's asleep and wonders if we could reschedule. It wasn't a good day for him."

"Sure," she said.

But then Tyler continued to her door.

"You're dropping me off?" she asked.

"I think that we've had enough of a night."

The fighter in Zoe urged her to walk past the cottage, toward the path to the cabins. He couldn't get off this easily.

But what would happen next if she pushed the issue?

Her breath came in shallow doses. "I'm still hungry."

"You want to go back in there?" He pointed to the big house, as if he wanted to get as far away from it as possible.

"How about you just walk me down to the cabins so we can see what's cooking with the guys?"

And she was off before he could say no.

Behind her, his boots crushed the gravel, and she

imagined he might be watching her walk. The fantasy of it brushed her skin, lifting her hairs on end with goose bumps.

Out of the desire to have him nearer, she slowed until he caught up, his shirtsleeve skimming her arm.

A team.

And…more?

As they marched in step, she got farther and farther away from that big mansion, her guesthouse…

And even how much her job had always meant to her.

This—the sunset, the way Tyler's steps matched hers—seemed so much more important.

She breathed him in. Saddle soap, leather. Everything she'd loved about the ranch when she was young.

Everything she loved now.

She looked up at him, and he glanced down at her, sending her heart into a jolt that it would probably never recover from.

"Maybe you were right about your father all along," she said.

"You mean about shining up his image?"

"Yes. Painting over who he really is could be a dis-service to you and your family." And her own. "If I detected more second thoughts in him or even a little sense of guilt, he'd be easier to work with."

"Like it's easier now with your dad."

She nodded. "I thought I saw an inkling of remorse in Eli. Then he blew that suspicion to smithereens."

Tyler looked ahead, into the distance, to where the sun kissed the edge of the pasture fences. "However I feel about my own father, he's not the main issue when it comes to maintaining the Barron image. Our family reputation also affects my brothers." He shoved his hands in his pockets. "It affects the families they might have someday."

A pain shot through her chest. "They?"

He stopped walking, just as Chance loped into view, then slowed, happy as could be running around.

While Tyler watched his horse, Zoe talked through the wet heat that began to prick at her eyes and throat. "You can have a family, too. Your ex-wife convinced you that you weren't suitable to have kids or keep a wife satisfied, but she was wrong. I've seen such things in you these past few days, Tyler. I see a *lot* of goodness even though I used to think differently. But I was wrong."

Very, very wrong.

Chance walked toward the fence, as if he sensed that Tyler was close.

"You're a fixer," Zoe added in a whisper. "Even tonight with your father… You were trying so hard to work through the harsh feelings with him until he put you in a place where you couldn't help defending yourself…and me."

How could she describe how it'd felt to hear Tyler coming to her rescue? She'd spent most of her life not needing that from a man, or from anyone, really, but having it now made her think that she'd finally done something to deserve it.

"See," he said. "That's why you're so good at PR, Zoe. You frame matters in just the right way."

"This isn't about PR." She shook her head. "Good heavens, you're stubborn."

Then she pulled him around so he was looking

down at her. His jaw was set, as if he didn't want to say anything more, but his eyes told her everything.

He was digesting each complimentary word of hers, maybe even coming to believe that he could have the same stature outside the office as in it.

And his gaze also told her that he felt something for her, whether or not he wanted to.

"You're a fixer," she repeated. "You have the talent to repair what's broken, whether it's a horse, your family…, yourself…"

She left the rest hanging, because she didn't want to say "me."

But it was true, wasn't it? He'd pulled something together in her.

Now she saw another message in his gaze. Was he thinking that they were alike? Two people who fixed. Two who'd been changed by the shifting faults in their families.

A pair who'd found another world here with each other.

When he bent to her, taking her face in his hands and pressing his mouth to hers with a yearning that echoed her own, Zoe melted once again, fusing their wants and needs together.

Ready to become a part of him in every way.

Chapter Nine

This kiss wasn't as experimental as the one at the swimming hole. It wasn't as innocent as the one he and Zoe had shared in the ballroom tonight.

This kiss was desperate, Tyler thought as he crushed her to him.

Inevitable.

While he kept one hand at her back, he slid his other to her nape, burying his fingers in hair so silky it was like dark rain. And as he kissed the corner of her mouth, then her cheek, he thought that her skin felt and tasted like the outside of a smooth fruit he was finally allowing himself to savor.

Then back to her lips…

Soft, wet, a temptation he couldn't resist, either.

She pulled at his shirt, stumbling backward, toward the edge of the path. He went with her, still holding on to her hair, his arm circling her waist.

When she took another step into the grass, his mind swam.

She wanted to go somewhere else—somewhere no one would see what they were doing.

More than a kiss…?

"Zoe," he murmured against her mouth.

In answer, she grabbed his shirt again, drawing it so far from him that the air caressed his belly, his chest. His stomach muscles hopped.

Their kiss slowed to a sinuous rhythm—him sipping at her, sucking, as if he could hold her here on the path, telling her without any words that they could still keep things safe between them.

But she kept leading him off that path.

"Where are you going?" he whispered.

"Old barn." She was all breath.

Privacy. Just the two of them alone, body to body.

Thumps of blood pummeled him, and in spite of every misgiving that clawed over his common sense, he scooped her into his arms.

No stopping this…inevitable…

She gasped as he started to carry her, the grass brushing his boots. She took a fistful of his collar, their gazes locking.

In her eyes, he saw the past as it hung over their stormy present…then the haze of a future he couldn't predict, except for the hope that she might be part of it.

Adrenaline swamped him, and he didn't know if it was because of fear or excitement—or maybe both. Either way, he pulled her so close that his heart thudded against her as he walked toward the old barn, which loomed against the flushing horizon. Zoe rubbed her face against his neck, her breathing warm. Moist. Cuts of air against his skin that drove him crazy.

Urging him to keep walking.

To get there.

Get there *now*.

When he stepped into the barn, Zoe was still just as passion-driven as he was, and she wriggled out of his arms, falling away while keeping an arm looped around his neck, dragging him down with her. She kissed him, grabbing his shirt again with one hand until he heard seams rip.

But where did she want to go from here?

He sure as hell wasn't about to continue matters on the ground of a barn, even if it was abandoned. Zoe deserved more: a big, soft, luxurious bed. Candlelight dinners. A view from a terrace.

But as she pulled him toward a stall, she stopped kissing him, smiled up at him.

What he saw was a lady unlike any he'd ever known before.

She was one who could send him spinning just by wearing a simple sundress, her skin glowing with a tan from walking outdoors or going to a swimming hole.

His most basic fantasies come to life in a woman.

Her eyes were wide—that beautiful sheen of dusky blue that seemed all the lighter because of her skin. Her lips were swollen because of his kisses.

His Zoe.

Around them, the scent of hay seemed like a memory of times gone by—of the games they'd played as kids here in the barn. She brought him into the stall, which had been stripped of accoutrements, empty except for the burnished slants of dusk coming through the walls.

But in Tyler's eyes, Zoe filled it right up.

She leaned back against the wall, and as she looked up at him, his heart—the one he'd rediscovered only lately—folded around the edges, like a page from a notebook scrawled with sweet nothings.

Did Zoe see these soft feelings in him—scribbled love poems that had never quite made sense until now?

Tyler's heartbeat jammed, as if it had stopped altogether and didn't know how to go on. But when she smiled at him again, he forgot about everything except for her.

"Tyler," she said, as if experimenting with his name. As if it sounded different to her when they were alone, where they could pretend that nothing else was waiting for them outside these walls.

He touched his fingertips to her face, tenderly, almost in disbelief, and she closed her eyes, her lashes dusting her skin.

Hunger for her surged through him, coming to churn in his belly. His groin.

He pressed his hand to the small of her back, bringing her to him, and he kissed her again. She moaned against his mouth, clearly knowing just what she did to him, how she affected every cell, every fiber.

Her leg snuggled against his, and as he drew at her mouth, he slid his hand under her thigh, raising her so that she was up against him even closer.

Harder.

She seemed to lose the ability to breathe, leaning her head back, grabbing at his shirt.

"Tell me when you want this to stop," he said, strangled, hoping she'd want him to go on and on. "Just tell me, Zoe."

"Do you have...something with you?"

A condom. He reached into his back pocket, brought out the wallet, dropped it, held up the package.

She dug her fingers into his hair, making him look into her eyes.

"Then why would I want you to stop?" she asked.

There'd been a lot of reasons before, but now there was such heat in her gaze that the flames seemed to blast into Tyler, too, eating up every last ounce of the common sense that had already been shredded within him.

He shoved the condom into a shirt pocket, then ran his thumb over her lips, down her chin, his hand traveling her neck, to the swell of her breasts under the innocent bodice of that dress.

While he traced his fingertips over the rise of them, her breasts rose and fell. She was so beautiful, so perfectly put together, and with every passing, pounding second, the blood throbbed lower, making him harder.

She arched, reaching in back of her to take care of her zipper.

"Let me," he said, taking over for her.

The buzz of the zipper dominated the sounds of the night, the clamor of Tyler's heartbeat. It even undid *him* as he brought the zipper lower.

Lower.

When he was finished, her bodice gaped, and she looked up at him through her lashes, suddenly shy.

How long had it been since *she* had taken a real lover?

He didn't have much time to think about that, because desire seemed to seize her, glazing over her gaze as she reached up and pulled down the straps of her dress, revealing a lacy bra underneath.

As if they were picking up where they'd left off at the swimming hole, she undid the clasp.

The slants of light made her golden, warming her smooth skin, the firm breasts tipped by dark pink nipples that had already pebbled.

Tyler rested his hands on her ribs, and she sucked in a long draft of oxygen. She held her breath as he stroked upward, cupping her breasts, sketching his thumbs over the dusk of their centers. He coasted around her nipples, making them stand harder.

She moaned, raising her hands overhead against the stall wall.

Her eager response made Tyler feel as if he was rising back to the top of the world, just where he thought he'd been before everything had tumbled down around him.

He bent to her, taking one breast in his mouth, working her nub around with his tongue, sucking at her, making her strain against him, her fingers digging into his shoulders. Her dress slid down and down, relaxing around her hips now.

Impatient, he yanked the material down farther, and she stepped out of it, clumsily, feverishly.

As she clutched him to her, he used one hand to pull at her panties—more lace, more innocence, more of the sublime simplicity that Zoe had brought into his life.

Soon, she was completely bared to him, breathtaking in the falling strips of light coming through the walls.

All *his*.

When he took off his clothes, too, he laid them on the ground, making the best bed he could. Then he lowered their bodies to those makeshift sheets, hoping this would be good enough for her—that she wasn't dreaming of making love with him in the big house instead...

He banished the thoughts as he sat, bringing her into his lap, her flesh against his own—smooth, damp with the sweat they'd been working up.

As he held her by the hips, he checked her gaze to see if there was any wariness there.

Not a bit.

He adjusted her so that she was straddling him, and when he slid his fingers through the moist folds between her legs, she clutched his upper arms, biting her lip.

Ready. She was so ready for *him*.

He slipped his fingers into her, and she gasped, closing her eyes and rising up, moving with him, still biting her lip, her head tilted to the side. Just watching her made him heat through more and more, and as his fingers went in and out, her hips churned, her moan rose, turning into a high groan until he couldn't stand any more.

Withdrawing, he reached for his shirt, getting that condom. Sliding it on. Then he circled an arm around her, laying her down, cushioning her with that arm while using his other hand to wrap her leg over him.

Then, with an easy stroke, he entered her.

The sound that had been building in her became a

full-fledged cry, and she grasped at him, burying her face in his neck.

They rocked together, him pushing into her, her urging him on. The world seemed to spin around them, faster, harder. Every move caused something inside him to rise even higher, far past where he'd ever been before in his life.

He was looking down on the world from this terrifying, ecstatic height, and Zoe was *still* with him, keeping him afloat.

Fuller, lighter, almost to the point where he would blow right open with one more sharp pulse of his heart.

It was too much, and he ripped open, free-falling backward, seeing Zoe right above him, reaching for him as he went down...down...

It seemed like eons before he hit a wall with a shudder so brutal that it felt like an explosion.

And as he came out of the mist, Zoe was there again, in his arms, all his.

Just as he was all hers.

As night fell, the light coming through the barn walls had turned to darker, soft colors that reminded Zoe of the haze in a crystal ball.

She was draped over Tyler, her cheek to his chest as they lay on his tangled clothes. Even though Tyler had tried to be a gentleman, making a bed for them, the material hadn't stopped dirt from getting on their damp skin.

But she didn't mind a little earthy grit.

Didn't mind at all.

She breathed him in, the scent of work, musk. She

wished he would say something. She was still halfway
on cloud nine, but she could catch glimpses of the old
Zoe on a lower plane, wondering whether she'd been
good enough for Tyler Barron.

And wasn't that just perfect? After making love to
the man, she was a ball of nerves.

The anxiety made her break the silence, the calmed
pace of their breathing.

"So much for my born-again virginity," she said.
Making light of this seemed way better than the wondering. Better than mulling over whether she'd made a
mistake and rushed things between them.

He curled her hair around his fingers, and his voice
hummed through his chest, against her skin. "How long
do you have to stay away from sex to qualify as a born-
again virgin?"

"Pretty long." She traced a circle on his chest. "A
few years at least."

In this afterglow, it was easy to believe that maybe
she'd even been waiting for this night forever—that
she'd been meant for Tyler and no one else.

"I'm glad this happened," she said.

"Me, too."

Only two words, but for some reason, Zoe thought
they could fill an entire epic novel. There was a hint of
profound emotion in his voice.

"I suppose we should get dinner," she said, but that
wasn't what she really wanted.

"Dinner would be good."

Yet he wasn't letting go of her, and she wasn't making
any sort of move away from him.

In fact, he wrapped his other arm over her, as if he
was going to stop her from going anywhere.

The possessive gesture got Zoe, deep and low, and she held him closer, too, nuzzling his chest.

Heaven. Surely this was what it would be like.

"I can hear your heartbeat," she said as it pounded beneath her ear. "It sounds like a big drum in a symphony. Except drums are hollow."

His fingers tightened on her.

She looked up to find him staring at the barn's roof, his gaze distant.

"Tyler?"

"Yeah?"

"What I meant to say is that *you're* not hollow. Sometimes I think you like people to believe your heart got scooped out a long time ago. But it survived."

"Hearts," he said, rolling her all the way on top of him, where she had a full view of his face.

His gaze was getting lust-steeped again, and it shivered her skin.

But what did his heart have to do with lust?

At that moment Zoe knew that having him wasn't enough. She wanted everything—his heart, his mind, each one of his coming days and nights. And *everything* didn't include any big, lovely mansion, either. It didn't mean that she needed to be the cream of the crop in her chosen field of business, where she could show the Barrons she was just as good as they were.

In fact, if being with him created a conflict of interest in business, she would give it all up for him.

Did he want that, too?

Or had he been crushed too many times to ever be whole enough for someone like her to love?

He was getting aroused beneath her again, but she wanted to see that special quality in his eyes that would surely show her what it meant to be loved back. And she thought she saw a glimmer of it.

Yet, just like that, as he coaxed his hands up the backs of her thighs, the look in his gaze turned into pure, heart-thundering desire.

For now, she gave in to it, thinking she still had enough time to show Tyler that he would have it in him to love someone again.

And, make no mistake about it, that someone was going to be her.

Tyler had walked Zoe back to her guesthouse, where they'd eaten some food from the pantry, fallen into bed again, then made love one more time. They'd drifted to sleep afterward, until just before dawn, when he'd slipped outside.

And it wasn't because he didn't want anyone to know he'd been with Zoe, holding her, exploring everything he wanted to know about the body that enthralled him. It was because...

Hell. Why would he make some kind of announcement to the ranch by flaunting where he'd been last night when he and Zoe were meant to end so soon? Because it would end, just after his family announced in a couple of days that Chet would be a copresident of The Group.

Then Zoe would be busier than a queen bee supervising her hive while she troubleshot and minded the media. She would probably even forget about her time on the ranch with Tyler altogether. She would move on, going to even bigger and better places while he did whatever he was going to do with the rest of his life.

After he'd gotten cleaned up, he came back to the

guesthouse, just as if he hadn't been there a couple hours earlier. She'd told him she would meet him here just before they went to the big house to say hi to Uncle Abe, as she was supposed to have done last night before Eli had shown up.

When she opened the door, she stole a beat out of Tyler's pulse.

She was in full business mode, wearing her hair slicked back and flipped up, garbed in a smart, fashionable maroon dress with capped sleeves and a high, belted waist. Her heels had straps that encircled her ankles, and Tyler gave in to a moment of fancy, imagining his fingers around a slim ankle, skimming upward, over her shapely calf, and up higher still...

She noticed that *he* noticed, and she colored up more than ever, maybe because she knew that he would live up to the vows of his hungry gaze if she let him. Or she could very well have been remembering last night, with him inside her...

"Hi," she said, almost shyly.

"Hi."

His voice had come out rough, and he hooked his thumbs through his belt loops. What did you say to a woman you'd known pretty damn well the night before? One you were beginning to care about more than you should?

They stood there until she got a dreamy sort of smile, then glanced away, as if letting him know that she was aware of how awkward this was and she wasn't going to make it any worse right now.

"What's on the agenda today after you meet with Abe?" he asked.

Business. The safest ground.

Was she disappointed?

Tyler couldn't quite tell.

"Jeremiah's coming out here today for a prerecorded interview with Fox Business Channel," she said.

"He told me something about an interview." Tyler almost kicked at the step in front of him but refrained. "Jer told me that you'd be conducting it near the stables, just for some picturesque family-type flavor."

"Exactly. I want him out of the corporate world and in a more natural one. In exchange for an exclusive chat, my reporter promised to sit on the news until the upcoming announcement. The channel's going to break the story first, accompanied by the interview."

If he'd thought she was okay with the direction of their talk before, he wasn't so sure now. Her gaze had clouded, as if covering up what she really wanted to be chatting about with him.

Tyler's chest seemed to squeeze, attempting to hide everything inside, just as he'd always done.

But now, standing here with Zoe, it just didn't feel right.

How else should he handle this, though?

He shot a lowered gaze at her. "Are you going to try to talk me into joining Jer for the initial media splash?"

Zoe reached behind her to close her door, and that pretty much shut out what had gone on in there—and the old barn—last night.

"I won't lie," she said, all businesswoman now as she stayed on that top step. "It's up to you. I've been hoping you'd come around to participating, but Jeremiah volunteered for this interview. Even with all the gossip he's causing, he told me he's the most levelheaded brother at the moment and he'd be best for the job."

"And he's right. He works off some steam at night, but in the office, he's steady. He and I talked about him taking the reins on this already, and I'm fine with him being the public face of the company."

He and his brother had also talked about what place Chet would have in this PR scheme, since their cousin—half brother—had refused to get involved in selling it so far.

Zoe brushed at her skirt, as if whisking away this conversation. "You ready?"

Her question seemed loaded, and Tyler wanted to tell her that he wasn't ready, after all.

She walked with him to the big house, and he smelled that lotion on her again—the kind that made him think of paradise and lapping water over sandy beaches.

He shut out the scent before he completely lost his mind and swept her into his arms, taking her back into her guesthouse to make love to her for the rest of the day.

When they entered Abe's room, where his uncle was poking at his breakfast from a tray in bed, Tyler was grateful that they weren't alone anymore.

Even though his uncle looked a bit washed-out today, he was alert enough to catch Tyler giving Zoe one last glance.

Abe grinned.

Dammit. He'd seen it—the way Tyler couldn't get Zoe out of his mind, out from under his skin.

"Abe," Tyler said. "You remember Zoe Velez. She's spearheading the PR campaign."

"I know just who Zoe is." Abe said it like there was an entirely different meaning to his comment.

And there probably was.

He extended his hand to her, and Zoe went to shake it before he could make the effort to get out of bed. Tyler watched him closely, thinking that Abe didn't seem to have enough strength to even get him that far.

He kept his eye on his uncle as Zoe said, "So glad to see you again."

Abe held on to her hand. His voice seemed weaker, too. "Jeremiah sent me a computer file of that new commercial. Nice job. I'd like to talk to you about what I can do in this campaign, too."

From Johnny the nurse's corner of the room, Tyler heard a grumble.

"Give it a rest, Chewbacca," Abe said to him. He addressed Zoe. "I call him that because he makes a lot of protesting sounds that only a few can translate."

Zoe sent Tyler a grin, and he read it well. Abe reminded her of her dad with all his affectionate grumbling.

"So," Abe said, and with that *so,* Tyler got all kinds of bad feelings. But at least Abe seemed more energetic now. "How've you been enjoying your return to the ranch, Zoe?"

"It's been fantastic," she said. "Almost like a working vacation."

"It's been nice to see Tyler having a little fun again, too."

Tyler cut his uncle off at the pass. "I guess we should let you finish breakfast, Abe. Zoe just wanted to say hi to you."

"Nonsense. Company's good for me, right, Johnny?"

The nurse spoke up. "Today, I'd prefer—"

"Stay a bit," Abe said, casting his keeper the stink eye.

Better to be safe than sorry with Abe. If he needed rest, he should get it.

"Zoe's got a full day ahead of her," Tyler said. "We can't keep her here for long."

Did she slump a little at that?

"Too bad." Abe carefully dabbed at his mouth with his linen napkin. "Being here on the ranch is a good time to slow down. You can stop to smell the flowers in the garden, listen to the birds... Zoe, have you wandered through the gardens out back?"

"I'm afraid I haven't had the opportunity."

"Then I insist that we have cocktail hour there when you can."

What was Abe trying to do here?

One look from his uncle filled Tyler in: Abe had seen the change in Tyler, and he'd attributed it, at least in part, to Zoe.

As Abe went on talking to her, Tyler got to thinking about that. How much of his new lease on life was due to being back in the country where he belonged?

And just how much of it really was due to the woman he was falling for a little more each day?

Chapter Ten

Zoe was damned if she was going to let Tyler go so easily.

Even after a long day of work, she found enough energy to set up a private dinner with him. Mrs. Nissan, the head cook, had been all too happy to whip up a meal for them; Zoe only wished she'd had time to do it herself, just out of pride, really, since she wanted to show Tyler that not only could she run a crackerjack PR campaign—she could be a domestic goddess, too.

She could balance all of it, in spite of her previous fears of crossing a professional line.

Yet there were only so many hours in a day. And there were also a whole lot of coworkers who had descended on her guesthouse, using it as a war room for tomorrow's scheduled media bombshell. She could barely navigate her kitchen, much less the living room, with all the files, cots and bodies sitting around.

So Zoe had brainstormed this little plan.

She inspected the old barn, which she'd illuminated with a few electric lanterns that created a soft glow at twilight. There was a linen-covered table, two chairs, a cooler and a couple of covered trays with all the gourmet delicacies she wanted to share with Tyler.

Things always had a way of working out for the best, she thought. The old barn was more romantic than the guesthouse for a dinner for two, anyway.

It was the place where she and Tyler had first made love.

As she sat in one of the folding chairs, she smoothed her maroon dress over her thighs. Then, unable to help herself, she looked at the stall.

Even now her body blazed with memory—his lips, his hands fitting her every curve, knowing all of her...

A shuffle of cowboy boots at the barn's entrance made Zoe refocus.

Was he here already? And had he caught her staring at the stall while wearing a dopey smile?

Before she turned to him, she said a tiny prayer that he would find her la-la-land haziness endearing.

Or would he be as cool as he had been earlier today?

Then again, maybe *cool* wasn't the word. She'd seen the heat in his gaze whenever he'd looked at her.

She found him standing at the entrance, a shadow against the bruised sky. The lantern light breathed over him, golden and reverent.

Or could it be that this was just how *she* saw him?

"You made it," she said.

"How could I ignore that note you left on my door? '8:00 p.m., old barn, good vittles and company'?"

She'd thought about leaving a saucier message, but there was something that told her she might still scare Tyler off, even with the way he'd been with her last night.

Gentle, then passionate...

Gesturing toward the seat opposite her, she told herself not to come on strong now, either, even though she had an agenda for inviting him here.

As he walked in, he doffed his Stetson, holding it in front of him like an old-time sheriff who said his share of ma'ams and misses. He set his hat on a crate near their stall without even acknowledging the landmark.

Was he ignoring it on purpose? Or was he just as aware of it as she was?

By the time he sat opposite her at the table, resting his forearms just above the knees, she'd taken the salad out of the cooler, unwrapped it.

As she tossed the greens, he asked, "How did you manage to get all this put together with the schedule you have?"

"Mrs. Nissan took care of the food. I had Ginnifer, my intern, load some stuff from the kitchens into a pickup, and I drove that down here."

"Here," he said, as if finally acknowledging the reason she'd chosen this old place.

"Yeah," she said. "*Here*. I figured we could be alone again." *Don't push it...* "Just to talk."

He hadn't bolted yet, so she put some salad in his bowl. "I'm taking a break for dinner, but then it's back to the grindstone."

"I saw some cars still parked in front of your guesthouse. Is your team waiting for you?"

"Yup. They're camped out, ready for the news cycle to start tomorrow. We've got to be up and running with it. I've got other coworkers in the city, though, closer to The Group's headquarters." She pointed a salad tong to the iPhone resting on the table, near her entrée plate. "I have to be ready to run if the team needs me, just until this entire storm passes."

She offered him vinegar and oil, and instead of using them on his salad first, he dressed hers. The thoughtful gesture tugged at her, but he was quiet. Almost too quiet.

He finally said, "Just in case I haven't mentioned it before, thanks, Zoe."

"For dinner? We all have to fill up."

"Not only for this. For making everything run smoothly. For treating my family with the decency you would've extended to your own."

A ring of warmth expanded in her. "It's been my pleasure."

And she meant that in so many ways. She only wished there was a guarantee that the pleasure would go on and on...

She dug her fork into her salad. Here went nothing.

"If anything, it was good to see you opening up during your time here on the ranch," she said. "I get the feeling you only needed someone who'd listen unconditionally."

It was just unfortunate that he had closed up a little with her this morning, as if removing himself was the only way he could figure out what had gone on between the two of them last night.

"I blossomed right up, did I?" he asked with an amused edge to his voice.

He seemed to think himself incapable of it or something. "You know what I mean. When I first saw you at the fair, I expected you to just keep to yourself. And you looked like you were about to fly into pieces, explode."

"Then maybe I have come along since then."

He sent her a meaningful glance, his eyes a deep green in the lantern light.

Was he attributing some of his improvement to her?

He transferred his gaze to his fork, the tines speared with greens. "In fact, I know I've come a long way. Anger used to seem like the safest place for me, but it's not. And it's a credit to you that I realize it."

She was so overcome she didn't know what to say besides, "I'm glad I could help."

They finally lifted their food to their mouths, eating, but Zoe didn't feel much closure about anything with him.

They'd only gotten started.

She swallowed her food, then realized that she hadn't poured the wine.

Getting it out of the cooler, she said, "As I was saying, you've opened up, so that's why I was slightly caught off guard this morning when you seemed…"

He'd stopped eating.

"…shut down," she finished.

Suddenly, he looked as if he wanted to be anywhere but here.

Great. But she'd put it out there. Now she would have to own it.

"I suppose I'd just like to get a feel for what last night meant in the scheme of things," she said.

Last night—it seemed to bring a flare of memory back to his gaze as it went hazy.

Zoe couldn't breathe as she waited for him to help her out here, to give her an answer one way or another. She was a big girl. She could take it.

Couldn't she?

A grin pulled at his lips, and he shook his head.

"You're blowing this off," she said.

"No." He went for more salad. "I'm relieved, actually. Thank God for your straight talk."

"Right, thank God—so why are you dancing around it?"

"Because I'm not used to someone calling me out on these personal matters. Usually, everybody around me outside of business waits until things snowball and, by then, it's too late for talk. You seem to know how to resolve issues early on, before they spiral out of control."

She only wished she'd known how to do this magic act when her parents had needed it.

"You haven't answered my question," she said.

"Yeah. Your question."

Struck speechless—that was what he was. But all she had to do was look into those eyes to see that maybe, just maybe, he wanted to say that last night had meant everything to him.

She felt as light as a balloon that someone had let go of at a fair, just to watch it fly. But she kept her tongue.

Every bit of logic in her offered a reminder. *Don't*

push him too far. If you give him another shove, it'll be in the wrong direction.

She turned her attention to a corkscrew, using it on the wine bottle. "Don't worry—I won't grill you about this anymore."

"No—you have every right to."

She could sense the struggle in him: if he told her what his eyes so clearly said, he would commit himself. Then he might fall short on that commitment, as he'd done with his ex, and as his mother had done with his father, and as Abe had done with Aunt Laura.

And this time, it might be the very last straw for Tyler.

Twisting the cork out of the bottle, she poured for him, then her. The liquid shone in the glass. She tried not to feel dull in comparison. Tried not to believe that he hadn't chosen her over all his ghosts.

Then, out of the corner of her eye, she saw Tyler rise from his chair, lean across the table. She felt him tip his finger under her chin, leading her to look at him.

When she did, adrenaline spiraled through her.

"I'm getting used to this all over again," he said softly. "And it's something I'm not very good at."

"But you *are* good." Sounded saucy—but she hadn't meant it in a wanton way. "What I'm trying to say is that during my time on the ranch, I've seen that you're truly good, Tyler, through and through. And I'm not asking for any kind of commitment from you—Lord knows, the mere thought of one makes my own heart just about want to sprint away from me—but..."

She stopped herself. She *did* want a commitment, more than anything. A true one, not just a sexual, I'm-not-going-to-let-him-get-away-that-easily vow.

Jeez, if she wanted a deeper commitment, how could she even say it?

How could she take it if he shot her down?

Tyler watched her patiently. "Go on."

He wasn't bolting off like some wild animal who'd been spooked. He was still here, touching her under the chin, making her look into his eyes.

She gripped the wine bottle. Courage.

This was what she wanted, and she could either reach out and try to grab it or...

Or she could not push him.

"What I'm getting at is this—if you need some time to give me an answer, that's how it'll be. I probably won't even be able to see you in the next few days, anyway, because of the media bomb." She steadied herself. "But you'd be worth waiting for if you decided that last night won't be the final one between us, after the scandal has blown over."

As he kept his finger under her chin, the adrenaline zipped around her, making the lantern light, the sight of wine and food on the table, surreal. She'd never gone out on a limb this far for anyone, and it felt as if everything might crumble beneath her.

He seemed to know that, and he bent farther over the table, using his finger to urge her chin forward.

Almost as if he was pulling her back from the edge.

Then he laid a tender kiss on her lips.

Zoe savored it, her mouth tingling. "Was that a definitive answer?"

"Did it give you what you need for now?"

She nodded, smiling. "Yeah. For now."

"Then it's answer enough."

He sat down, clearly gaining some kind of appetite as he started to eat again.

Content.

Comfortable.

That was what she'd wanted for him, and it was good enough for her.

For now.

They were just starting the main course of trout wrapped in foil and baked with garlic, lemon and jalapeños when Zoe's phone vibrated on the table.

Tyler's posture tightened, and Zoe remembered that even though they were in a barn, on a ranch, seemingly away from everything, the world would always be right outside.

She glanced at the caller ID screen. One of her PR team members.

"Mind if I take it?" she asked.

Tyler's nod was stiff, and although he tried to grin again, he'd seemed to lose hold of the carefree cowboy who'd been eating dinner with her.

As she walked away from the table, answering her call, she felt his mind and heart wandering a step away from her, too.

When the bomb dropped on the business world about The Barron Group's new family/corporate order, it did so in such a controlled way that Tyler merely had to hold on instead of praying for his family's lives.

Walker & Associates definitely had matters well in hand, having leaked the story to the board and stock-holders even before Jeremiah's interview aired that morning and the dogs of journalism came sniffing around. It could've been tabloid hell for the Barrons if not for the damage control the PR firm performed over the next few days.

All the while, Tyler had stuck to his cabin; he and his infamous temper had been kept from public interviews. But Jeremiah had been masterful at being the primary public face of the company.

Just as masterful as Zoe—the woman behind it all.

Still, she hadn't been able to round up the rest of the Barrons here on this ranch, as she had hoped to do. Jeremiah was the only one who'd elected to stay in the big house. Chet and Eli had decided to spend their time out of town, although, according to all accounts, they weren't battening down the hatches together. Chet was still in Utah, sans Eli, planning to get back to the ranch again in a few days when new headlines took over the old.

And now that the initial rush was over, Tyler was spending the day trying to find some time with Abe, who was sleeping so much that Tyler couldn't keep a measure of concern from hounding him. Even now, after sunset, he was waiting in the gardens for Johnny to summon him and give his blessing for just a short "hi" to his uncle.

But Tyler was here for someone else, too.

He'd taken a seat at a wrought-iron table near the paths filled with azaleas, magnolias and wisteria. He had a velvet gift box with him—a token of appreciation that had been delivered to the big house about an hour ago.

He ran a thumb over its smoothness. Only a trinket, he thought. Only a sign of the family's appreciation for what Zoe had accomplished for them, and he meant to give it to her tonight since she would finally have a moment free.

But gift giving didn't exactly explain why his pulse was pistoning.

He'd missed her, and that scared the life out of him.

When she finally arrived in the gardens, he had iced tea and teacakes waiting. Even at first glance she had him all tied up: Zoe, with a withered burgundy jacket draped over an arm. The collar of her sleeveless white blouse gaped open, as if she'd undone an extra button and packed business away for the night.

Happiness rose in Tyler—the pleasure of seeing her again. The excitement of being near enough so he could reach out and touch her if he dared.

He'd put the gift box on the chair next to him, hiding it as he poured her some iced tea from a pitcher.

"You read my mind," she said, taking the mint-sprigged glass from him and gulping down the drink.

He watched her throat work and barely stopped himself from saying to hell with it all and taking her in his arms.

Too soon. Too...

What? They'd already gone to bed together. It was what came next that made the hairs on his skin rise.

As if he could avoid that "what came next" forever, he oh-so-casually put the gift box on the table, sliding it over to her.

She set down the iced tea, and the mint leaves that'd been perched at the rim fell to the table.

"What's this?" she asked.

He shrugged. How could he put it into words?

This is what I'm giving you instead of my heart—for

*now. This is something I didn't have to cut out of me,
but it means a lot just the same....*

"Open it," he said.

She did, the hinges creaking. Then she paused just
before pulling out a Swarovski snow globe with a horse
just like Chance in the middle.

She merely stared at it for what seemed like a full
minute.

Did she think it was cheesy? Inappropriate?

"I can have it returned if—"

"It's beautiful," she said. Then she cleared her throat.
"It's...valuable."

He was about to tell her that money was nothing, but
then she turned her gaze to him. As she swept over his
cowboy garb, he realized that she hadn't been talking
about money at all.

This gift contained everything he'd been when he
was a boy—a horse, hope, floating dreams. It was valuable because it really *was* him, even though he hadn't
meant that—at least not consciously—when he'd found
the gift online.

Or maybe he *had* known it, and this was what he'd
given her instead of what he knew she really wanted.

The real boy who'd become this man.

She turned the globe upside down, shaking it, sum-
moning the snow, then set the object upright on the
table. The flakes swirled around the horse, obscuring
it.

"It's beautiful," she repeated. "You didn't have to do
this. Really."

"I had to do something to show how grateful we are
to you. You can keep this for a long time, look at it when
you want, remember..."

She laughed hurtfully. "You don't have to go on."

He leaned forward in his chair. "Do you think I changed my mind and I'm kissing you off?"

"You're...not?"

He took in her confused gaze, the knit of her brow.

Good God, Zoe wasn't just talking about a fling with him, was she? She hadn't said it in so many words, but from the way her heart shone in her eyes, she wanted more out of him.

Wanted all of him?

Panic should've made him fly right out of there, but it didn't. No, he stayed put, even though he had no idea just how that was possible.

But as the seconds passed, her obvious affection for him sank in.

More than sex.

Love...?

The very idea rocked him to his foundations, but after the initial shock, he realized he was still in one piece.

And he hadn't run off yet.

He was still here, feeling something revolving in him, warming him up, bit by bit.

"I'm not breaking up anything here, Zoe," he finally whispered. But he wasn't sure what else to say, or if he should even say it if it came to him.

He shook his head as the silence grew. "God, what poor communication skills I have. Some tycoon, huh? Masterful in the boardroom and that's about it."

"Tyler." She'd leaned forward, too. "Stop thinking that you're only a business guy. You haven't really been one for a couple of weeks now."

And there it was—stated baldly and thoroughly.

He hadn't been the only one to see it.

The last of the snow drifted to the bottom of the globe, leaving the horse crystal clear. Leaving a lot else clarified, too.

Zoe tugged at his sleeve, and he took her hand, feeling the burn, the brand of her skin. Around them, the night hovered—crickets, fireflies, flowers.

Say something, he thought. *Even if you can't say it all.*

"I'm just glad you're still around," he said.

She smiled, her gaze going misty, as if she knew that he'd really been saying that he didn't want her to leave, not even when her work was done.

As if she knew that he would come around to saying more if she could just be patient with him.

Behind them, in the house, someone yelled, his voice carrying through an open window where filmy curtains lazily stirred.

Tyler didn't pay any mind to it, though. Zoe was here, and she had her hand in his. That was all he wanted right now.

But then Jeremiah ran out of the house, panting, slowing to a walk when he saw Tyler and Zoe sitting there.

Then he came to a complete stop.

They stared at each other from across the bushes, Tyler's pulse flailing because of the panic he saw in his brother's eyes.

Tyler slowly stood, and he was aware of Zoe doing the same thing right next to him.

"What is it, Jer?" he asked.

Jeremiah came closer, shaking his head. His eyes were wide, his forehead creased below that flop of dark blond hair.

"What?"

"Abe." Jeremiah shook his head. "Johnny can't revive him. He called 911. Abe won't wake up. He's…"

Tyler felt as if he was crumbling back into his chair but, somehow, he was still standing, refusing to believe what he was hearing.

Behind him, Zoe took him by the arm.

As Jeremiah just kept shaking his head, Tyler thudded into his chair.

Abe.

Gone.

Tyler sat there for a long time while Zoe took hold of him, an anchor. A support.

But, in time, his mind seemed to dig its way up through the ashes, unearthing thoughts that roiled.

Eli.

Abe would still be alive if it wasn't for what Tyler's damn father had brought on the family.

In spite of what Zoe had taught him about releasing the bitterness, Tyler wasn't going to let this go unpunished.

His old man had to pay.

A sense of déjà vu struck Zoe as Tyler tensed, just as if he was going to run off.

"Where's Eli?" he said through his teeth.

Jeremiah was still just where he'd stopped. "I don't know."

As she'd done before, Zoe held Tyler back before he could do something he regretted, like picking up a phone and taking all his agony out on his dad.

"Let go of me, Zoe," he said.

Ice cold. So cold that everything they'd shared—

these past few moments, the hope for what should and could come next for them—shattered.

The worst day of Zoe's life replayed in her mind—Mom packing their bags, putting Zoe in the car, then telling her not to look back as they drove away from the cabin, from the ranch and everything she'd held so dear here.

"Abe wouldn't want this," Zoe said. Jeremiah was slowly approaching the table, as if cautious about what his brother was going to do. "I know what you're thinking, and you're *better* than that."

Tyler turned on her, and it was a man Zoe didn't even recognize.

The distant tycoon, a world away from her. A... Barron.

"He killed Abe," the man said. "My *father* killed him. If he hadn't brought this on my uncle, he'd still be alive."

She wanted to tell him that he didn't know this was true. That Abe might've gotten cancer anyway and he couldn't blame Eli for that, no matter how much of a jerk he was.

But this wasn't the time. "Just go to Abe now. Say goodbye to him and forget about your dad until later."

"Forget?" He reared away from her. "*Forgive?* Is that what you're asking me to do?"

Then Tyler lowered his voice, becoming deceptively calm as he addressed Jeremiah.

"You go to Abe, Jer," he said. "I'll be along in a minute."

"You need to come, too, Tyler, before they cover him up and take him—"

Tyler added a forceful, *"Go."*

Jeremiah bristled, then left, as if knowing when to cut his losses.

When they were alone, Tyler continued in that eerily low, deceptively serene voice.

"Forgiving and forgetting... You know, Abe told me a little something about both of them. He said he forgave my dad and Aunt Laura, but I don't think he ever really did—not with how he made sure my father paid for his actions before Abe passed on. My uncle wanted to see a reckoning. And I think he was right to do it."

"But—"

"I know. I thought I might be able to put *my* hard feelings aside. For a while, I believed I could with all my heart."

She saw bare truth in his eyes. Maybe it *was* still in him to forgive, but the darkness in his pupils was expanding, swallowing up everything else.

She wanted to shake him, to bring back the Tyler she knew so she could chase off this angry, vengeful man who'd taken over and turned her Tyler the wrong way.

This wasn't the man she'd fallen in love with.

"You *can* do it," she said.

But she wouldn't plead with him.

Neither of them needed for that to happen.

He paused at the loving note in her voice. The tacit offer to do whatever she could to walk with him on the high road instead of the low.

As he stared straight ahead, trying to get hold of himself, she began to reach out again, to touch him as she always did, bringing him all the way back.

Then the sound of a siren from the nearby town of Duarte Hill wailed in the night, and he looked away from her, toward the house.

His jaw clenched, as if remembering Abe and what he'd gone through because of Eli Barron.

With all the bad timing of a harbinger, her phone buzzed, and Tyler stood up so abruptly, taking off to do what he thought he had to do, that he jarred the table.

The snow globe wobbled, and Zoe winced, seeing it tumble off the edge before he could catch it.

It smashed to the ground, splintering into pieces, just like that cocktail glass Eli Barron had thrown against the fireplace the other night.

Both of them just stood there, staring at the damage—the liquid pooling over the ground, the shattered horse in the midst of a storm of glass and fake snow.

Zoe's heart seemed to bleed, too, especially when Tyler said, "I'll buy you another one."

But as he strode toward the big house, a total stranger casting a long shadow behind him, Zoe knew that nothing could replace what had been broken.

Chapter Eleven

Nearly a week later, summer rain tapped against the window in Miguel's cabin as Zoe sat with her dad on his fake cowhide sofa. She and Ginnifer had spent the day transferring files and computers out of the guesthouse and back to the office in the city, and Zoe was beat.

But that wasn't all there was to it.

Her dad had some sort of fishing program on the TV, and he watched it while saying, "Is this your last night in the guesthouse then?"

"Yes." Zoe was holding one of her dad's knit blankets to her chest. In front of her, the screen flashed with scenes of fish on hooks. "No sense in my being there any longer since the scandal is…"

She'd been about to say "nearly dead," but she couldn't. Not with Abe's funeral coming up this weekend. There'd been a spike in news activity when he'd passed on—some subtle speculation in the media about how the scandal had perhaps hastened his demise—but, as always, she and her team had tamped it down.

Even so, it all left Zoe with a bad taste in her mouth.

Eli Barron, getting off scot-free again. Tyler, making certain he never forgave his dad for this final sin.

Her dad spoke. "You're not happy with yourself, are you?"

"Me?"

"Zoe."

She glanced over to find him running a concerned gaze over her and, suddenly, she felt like a girl who wasn't sure where to go, one who just wanted her father to give her advice, even if she was so used to doing everything on her own.

"Mija," he said. "You feel bad about Abe's death and perhaps about easing Eli's part in it."

"Abe got what he wanted out of his brother in the end, Poppy. I think he died a content man."

"Then your long face must have to do with something else."

She wouldn't make eye contact with her dad. If she did, the tears would come, and she'd been so good about holding them back night after night since Tyler had left her standing in the garden among all that broken glass.

Her dad continued in a quiet, comforting tone. "I don't know what was with you and Tyler, but now that he's moved out of his cabin and gone back to his place in the city, you're not the same. You don't have that smile, Zoe."

No use in hiding it.

Sorrow itched at her throat. "I hear Tyler's cleaning

out his office in the city. He left Chance here for Keith to take care of..."

And that was a tragedy to her. It was the sign of a man who'd learned nothing when she thought he'd come such a long way. A person who'd lost hope and had gone back to alienating himself, just as he had after getting decimated by his divorce. If she were to meet him now, she wasn't even sure she could look at him.

Then again, how would she know when she hadn't even called him? Sure, she'd checked up on him through Jeremiah and sent cards and heartfelt condolences, but that wasn't the same.

It was just that she was pretty sure Tyler wouldn't take her calls—not the Tyler she'd loved, anyway.

The rain kept needling the window, and it was as if the sharp drops were doing the same to her skin, poking underneath it.

Her dad reclined on the couch, his hands clasped over the slight mound of his stomach. "It seems that's all there is to talk about then. Who knows if we'll ever see him again—"

She flashed a hurt glance at him.

"A reaction. Now, that's more like it."

Then she sent her father a chiding look, but when she saw him grinning, she didn't have it in her to mean it. "You're just trying to get my goat."

"I'm trying to shake you out of this funk. I'll be damned if my firecracker daughter sits here on a couch, watching the rain splat against the windows, while there's still work to be done. Because that's what it would take, you know. Some hard effort."

"It?"

"Tyler, *mija*. Stop pretending he isn't tearing you apart."

When something seemed to shift in his dark eyes, Zoe read it well.

Her dad knew what it was like to see someone leave, and he didn't want the same for her.

"Poppy?" she said. "I never did thank you for wanting the best for us back then, even if it meant swallowing your pride."

His eyes welled up and he cleared his throat. Then he nodded, as if he didn't trust himself to speak.

A few moments passed. Men casting their fishing lines on the TV. Men reeling in their catches and finding their hooks empty.

Then her dad tried again. "Maybe I did the right thing back then by refusing to fight with Eli, but I did the wrong thing by letting your mother go. I should've battled more for her. I should've swallowed that pride of mine and won her back."

"By confronting your boss and knowing that you probably wouldn't find a better job in the state?"

"No. By letting her know that I understood why she was so angry. Or at least that I wanted to understand."

She sensed a double meaning in him. "I've done the same thing with Tyler. But he wants to hold on to that anger even more than he wants…me."

Having voiced the rejection—and to her father, of all people—Zoe leaned back her head, resting it on the sofa. She'd been let go by someone she loved once, when her dad had given her up, and this time, it was just as devastating.

No…*more*. Worse.

"Do you love him?" her dad asked.

Her face burned.

"Wait—you don't have to tell me that. But I suspect you at least like him quite a bit, Zoe—enough to sulk around your poppy's cabin like you're doing now. And if you do care about him that much, you might think about going after him. If your mom had known that I would've done anything to have her back, it might've been easier for her to turn away from her anger. But I never did let her know."

Zoe felt frozen. A lifetime of thinking that she wasn't good enough for anyone mired her in the certainty that, surely, she wouldn't be good enough for Tyler, either. She didn't have the power to nurse him or compete with his darker need to keep on hating.

But then she remembered how he'd looked at her, with those green eyes filled with a feeling she'd never seen in a man before.

Wasn't that enough?

If it wasn't, what the hell was?

She laughed, but it was more like a tight sob. All these years she'd been fighting to show that she was just as good as the Barrons—as everyone else, really. But lately, the fight had changed course.

She wanted to do battle for Tyler now. Wanted him to see that he could be a family man. *Her* family man. Nothing seemed more important than that now.

Nothing.

Her dad smiled, his face so much older and wiser than it should've been at his age.

"Don't let him get away," he said.

She smiled, too, her determination revving up, bringing Zoe back.

* * *

Tyler was standing in front of the long, floor-to-ceiling office window that presented a grand view of San Antonio. But rain shrouded his vantage point with dots of water on the glass, revealing only gray and black blurs that took the place of sky and city buildings.

He was looking for a hint of blue among the gray—the hue of smoky blue, to be exact. And just the thought of such a color made his heart pump. He wasn't sure why until the blue-gray enveloped his mind.

Zoe's eyes.

A pang hollowed him out, but he fisted his hands.

Zoe was the past.

And he would keep on telling himself that, especially since she hadn't contacted him after he'd abandoned her. Not that he'd expected her to chase him or anything. He'd left her just as surely as he'd left just about everything else about the ranch, including all those thoughts he'd had about forgiving and forgetting. There, everything had seemed so possible.

The only remnant he would be taking with him was Chance, and Keith had vowed to take good care of the horse while Tyler corrected his course yet again. He wanted to find a place with wide-open spaces, where Chance could live, too, maybe with other wounded creatures.

The rain seemed to mock Tyler, counting down to the future, when Eli would also inevitably be back for Abe's funeral.

Was Eli off somewhere, privately taking responsibility for Abe's death?

Was he finally getting a suitable punishment?

Tyler's intercom buzzed, and the voice of Stella, his assistant, filtered through.

"Jeremiah wonders if you've got a minute for him," she said in her pronounced drawl.

Tyler turned from the window. His office, with its sleek silver-and-glass desk and modern art paintings, didn't differ much from the rain-soaked view of the outside.

"Send him in."

Jeremiah eased through the door, leaving it ajar behind him for some reason. In front of him lay the half-packed boxes that Tyler was using to clean out his office for good.

"Just wanted to touch base with you."

Abe's death had thrown everyone for a loop, even the unflappable Jeremiah. Reportedly, he was drowning his sorrows with even *more* women every passing night.

Just one more person dear old dad had screwed up.

"What's going on?" Tyler asked.

"The *Wall Street Journal* is wondering if you'd do an interview."

"No."

Jeremiah sighed. "Guess they'll just have to go through the PR machine then."

At the mention of PR, Tyler switched off completely. He didn't want to think about Zoe. Didn't want to dwell on how many damn times he'd almost gone back to her to say he was sorry that he hadn't been the man she'd thought he was. That he obviously never would be.

Dammit, why couldn't he just shake her off?

Jeremiah still hadn't left.

"Anything else?" Tyler asked.

"Yeah." He went back to the door, opened it. "A lot else."

And there she stood.

Just like that day in the swimming hole, he didn't think she was real at first, and he drank her in.

Zoe, wrapped in a crocheted blue shawl, the folds of her flowered sundress rustling over her legs.

When she stepped through the doorway, Tyler fought the urge to brace his hands on the back of his chair. Instead, he kept himself upright as Jeremiah left the room and closed the door behind him.

She scanned Tyler, and he became all too aware of the jeans and boots he was wearing, just as if he'd never left the ranch. With every one of his choked heartbeats, he saw her gaze go sadder and sadder, as if she knew he was gone for good, despite his Western clothing.

His heart ached, but he swatted away the weakness in him. He was never going to indulge in it again by pretending a week or two in the country would solve everything.

"Did Jeremiah call you?" he asked.

"I've been calling him, just to see how you were doing. This time, he told me I should come here."

"Is this business-related?" he asked.

She flinched at that. But then she raised her chin, just as she always did when she was put in a corner. At her show of strength and vulnerability, his heart lifted, too, just before he squelched it back down.

"We've got business, all right," she said. "Unfinished, if you'll remember."

He lifted his hands in a half shrug, but she beat him to saying something. Then again, Zoe had embraced what she really was in their short time together—a deep-down country girl who told it like it was.

She came closer to his desk, which stood between them. "You could've spent that sabbatical anywhere in the world, but you came back to the ranch. Home. You found yourself there until life knocked you flat on your butt again and now you're gone, just like that."

"Well, I guess you know all about me."

"I guess I do." She wrapped the shawl tighter around her, just as she'd done by the swimming hole that one morning, with his towel. Strong, yet with a chink in that armor of hers.

What had she risked to come to him?

How hard had it been to take a chance on seeing him again?

At the thought that she might've put everything on the line right now—her heart, her pride—Tyler regirded himself. He didn't need anyone, because they always turned on him, whether it was in death or in life.

Zoe would be the same.

She kept standing there, daring him to leave. "Can you really tell me that you're happy?"

"Happiness is what you make of it."

"You didn't say yes."

"Yes, Zoe." He tried to put truth into his words. "I'm happy."

"If I really believed that, I'd be out the door. But I'm not going anywhere."

Every second was like a chisel to his skin, which had grown so tough. Every time she spoke, her soft voice hammered, getting below his surface.

"You really should go," he said, turning toward the

window again. If he kept looking at her, he would give in, and the leaving cycle would only continue.

And he couldn't stand for her to be the one who abandoned him this time.

"Anger's not going to protect you," she said, her voice wavering now. "You were raised to think that life should be perfect—that you should be, too—and until you see that it isn't—and that *you're* not—you're never going to be at peace with the world around you. You can't save everyone, Tyler, and they will let you down one way or another, whether it's something small or—"

"Something life-altering? Like everything that's happened in the past month?"

Including being with her?

Because Zoe was the one person who seemed to pull him out of the mire.

But what would he do if she couldn't manage it one day?

As he still faced the window, he could imagine her behind him, gripping the edges of that shawl, frustrated because he couldn't be swayed. If he were a different kind of man, he could take her hands, tell her that, in time, he could change. He could be happy.

But again and again, he'd found that it wasn't true.

"Tyler," she said, "I used to think like you. I used to cling to anger and thoughts of getting back at people. I realized that I wasted so much time on all that."

Her tone had gone really wobbly now, and it was beyond Tyler not to check on her.

Her eyes were watery, leaving a trail of tears on the cheeks he'd taken such pleasure in stroking. Seeing her like this, crying and brokenhearted, snapped Tyler apart.

"God," he whispered. "Just look what I do to you. You want even more of it? Because that's all you'd get."

"That's not true."

Now he could see that she was also crying because she was at her wits' end with him.

She was close to giving up on him.

No surprise.

"I sincerely doubt that I have it in me to make anybody happy," he said.

"*You* made me happy," she said. "Don't you remember?"

Kisses with Zoe...laughing with her as they held each other...her looking up at him after he rescued a horse, as if he was some kind of gold-star hero...

Tyler's heart banged at him, as if it was trying to get out of the box he'd shoved it in. Zoe had been the only one who'd ever really brought it out.

But he'd left it exposed for too long, and look what had happened.

"What matters," he said, "is that you're not happy now, and I'm telling you—"

She shook her head, just as Jeremiah had done on the night Abe had died. And maybe this was a kind of death, too. Tyler sure felt numb enough inside.

Didn't she understand that this was for the best?

She was backing away from him now, her head tilted as if she couldn't understand where he'd gone.

When she got to the door, she held on to the knob. "Even after all this, if you ever decide that this is no way to live, I'm still going to be there. I'm leaving you alone now, but I'm *not* going to be the one to really go."

In her eyes, he saw that flash of hero appreciation

again, but then she went out the door, pulling at Tyler's heart, as if taking it with her.

He got it back just in time, trying to force it into its deep-down hideaway.

But it was as if that damn heart wouldn't go back inside.

He shoved his office chair away, and a flood of safety shrouded him—the anger. The cocoon of it.

He tried to let it soothe him, but this time...

This time, it didn't.

As Tyler turned back to his view of the city, he realized that the rain had let up, and his heart began to beat, louder, more painfully than ever, seeming to fill a room that was so very empty without Zoe in it.

Zoe returned to the guesthouse, packing up everything but her necessities.

She would be staying here one more night and then she would be gone.

As she sat at the dainty, white wicker kitchen table, she picked at the frozen vegetable lasagna she'd thawed in the fridge. She'd told her dad that she wasn't up for dinner tonight, and he'd left it at that, making her promise instead that she would come back to visit every once in a while for other dinners.

She'd agreed.

That was one thing that had come out of her stay here, she thought. A better relationship with Poppy. And that was good enough.

It really was.

She set her fork down, peering around the kitchen. She would miss the gingerbread woodwork, the state-of-the-art appliances gleaming sparkly white. She would miss the little pond nearby, with its lily pads, miss the birds singing in the morning.

But she didn't belong here. Even if she lived in a cabin like her father, where she could go fishing in the creek if she wanted, where she could lie on the swimming hole dock in the morning and go on to ride through the meadows, she had no business on Florence Ranch.

Tyler had made her believe in the dream, but he was gone.

Gone in a lot of ways.

Her phone vibrated, and she glanced at the ID screen. A text message from one of the guys she'd met a few weeks ago online. They'd had some nice exchanges, and she'd even been thinking about having coffee with him sometime.

She left her phone alone, but it wasn't because she knew that anything she started up with the guy would be doomed to fail.

It was because she couldn't even think about any other man but Tyler. She doubted she ever would.

As the post-rain sky darkened her window, Zoe kept sitting there, telling herself she would get up in a few minutes.

Just as soon as her heart was in it.

Chapter Twelve

Tyler sat in his Jag, across the lane from his father's town house in Alamo Heights, near downtown San Antonio. The exclusive neighborhood was quiet.

The night was quiet, too, especially without the rain.

If you ever decide that this is no way to live, I'll be here.

Zoe's last words kept echoing through his mind, and he couldn't ignore them because they were so right.

He *had* to find another way.

And that was why he was here.

A black limo cut through the water slicking the lane, and it pulled into his dad's porte cochere. Tyler checked his watch. Before he'd left the office, Stella had told him that his father was on his way back to San Antonio.

It had been like a sign.

Tyler watched as the driver exited the limo, opening the back door and letting out Eli Barron.

His father's big, black coat seemed to envelope him as he pulled up the collar, hiding most of his graying dark blond hair, then walked to the entrance of his stone-and-ivy town house, where he preferred to stay during the week. But as he went inside, leaving the door open a little bit behind him, it looked as if the stately domain had also become a place of banishment.

No matter how much Tyler despised his father, there was still a son inside him. There had to be a genuine man there who had it in him to balance some forgiveness with strength, just as Zoe had done.

So why hadn't he stopped her from leaving his office?

A new weight settled on Tyler, but it was over his heart, which pulled and strained, as if trying to find a way back out.

But first, there was this. He had to make amends with himself before he would be any good to her.

Just as he got ready to open his own door, another person came out of the limousine and headed for Eli's town house.

Chet?

He was bundled under a sheepskin coat, his boots splashing through the puddles on his way to the door, his shoulders slumped under the burden of his baggage.

Had Eli gone to Chet in Utah? Had he gone after Chet to press his case?

Tyler waited while Chet went inside and the driver brought a few pieces of luggage into the house. Then, when the limo finally left, Tyler decided it was time.

He went to the door, knocked.

It took a while for anyone to answer, either because his dad was engaged in a conversation with Chet or because he'd seen Tyler on the security camera. Nonetheless, he eventually opened the door.

The first thing Tyler noticed was that his father seemed haggard. Everything had apparently caught up to Eli, leaving him with hair that needed a good trim, skin that seemed blotchy from too many late-night bouts with the bottle.

As his father just stood there looking at him, Tyler said, "If you're wondering how I got past the gates, the guard let me in."

"I never told him you weren't welcome."

He sounded just as tired as Tyler had been right after the big announcement. Maybe they were both too exhausted to fight with each other anymore.

Eli opened the door all the way, and Tyler walked in, dried his boots, then shed his coat before hanging it on a wrought-iron tree. The foyer didn't hold much more besides that, except for a mahogany bureau and Spanish tile flooring.

Relatively modest, kind of like Tyler's own city home.

Without waiting, his dad ambled past the stairway and toward his sunken living room. He dropped onto a leather sofa before the central fire pit, which was cold and blackened with the remnants of previous fires.

Tyler sat down in a chair across from his dad.

"I couldn't help noticing that Chet was in the limo with you," he said. Mild. No hint of accusation.

And it seemed to work.

Eli's body seemed shapeless against the cushions,

staring at the ceiling, sober as a judge today. "I took a detour to Chet's Utah development."

"How did it go?"

Eli slid Tyler an appraising glance, as if wondering whether this was the prelude to another free-for-all.

"It went as well as can be expected." His dad returned to fixating on the ceiling. "I only wanted to apologize to him, make sure he knew how sorry I am about Abe."

Tyler could hear genuine devastation and regret. And, as Zoe had said, it did make moving on to the next step easier.

Step by step, he thought.

"He came here with you," Tyler said. "That's a positive sign."

"He's up in a guestroom that I use to store mementos. Stuff from the old days with me and Abe, when the company first started. When we were young bachelors on the town. Pictures of us as kids. News clippings. I told Chet that he can take whatever he wants."

Tyler could just imagine Eli offering anything he could to get on Chet's good side.

The rest of his words didn't come easily, but he managed to get them out.

"It's obvious that Chet's your love child. That you might've had more feelings for Laura than you'll admit, and he's a result of them."

Eli closed his eyes, already giving up if this was going to be a call to arms.

Tyler continued. "I'm not saying this because I want to stick it in your face. It's just something I'll have to get used to."

Eli opened his eyes and frowned, not quite getting where Tyler was going.

He sighed. "I've started to come to terms with my part in all this—how I never gave much thought to what I wanted. How I gave it all up for your sake…the family's sake. And Abe's funeral is the day after tomorrow. I won't go there to celebrate Abe's memory while refusing to carry out what he wanted for Chet. I'm going to honor Abe's memory by bringing some peace to this family."

"You're accepting Chet as your brother?"

One last slap of bitterness worked its way down Tyler's arms, making him clench his hands.

One step at a time.

It might be a while before he could sincerely put this wish of Abe's into action, feeling like Chet was one of theirs. But he was at least going to act like it for now.

For Abe.

Tyler ignored the question and nodded toward the second floor instead. "He's up there?"

Eli only nodded, staring at the ceiling again.

At least he'd made a start with his dad, and Tyler left him, not chancing anything more.

He went up the stairs, his boots thudding, and when he found Chet in the guestroom, it was clear that the man had been expecting Tyler. He was sitting on the edge of the king-size bed, still wearing his sheepskin coat, his hat. Next to him, a big plastic file box waited.

"Eli had these out already," Chet said.

Tyler got his meaning. Eli had been looking through the mementos in private.

Mourning his brother.

Tyler didn't ask himself whether or not Eli had experienced any anguish during the process, because Chet had a picture in his hand, offering it to Tyler.

As he accepted it, he didn't glance at the photo right away. All he saw was Chet with his hat drawn low, nearly shading his eyes. Still, it was enough for Tyler to see the redness surrounding Chet's irises.

Something pushed at his chest from the inside out, and he realized what it was. The responsibility of being a big brother.

A purpose.

As he got used to this feeling with Chet, he glanced at the photo—a faded Polaroid. Abe in his slick yet modest suit, Eli in his college graduation robes. Both with ridiculous, too-long hair. The original brothers Barron with their arms around each other, pumping their fists, the whole world ahead of them.

Chet's voice was scraped. "He looked so young."

Tyler knew what Chet meant.

Fresh-faced. Optimistic. Thinking that he was going to have life by the tail.

Chet went on. "I've been sitting here wondering what it would've been like to meet him back then. Would we have had more in common? Was he different from the man I turned away from when I decided that a ranch in Montana was more important than him and my mother?"

"You didn't think that." Tyler held on to the picture. "Abe raised you to go and get what you wanted, and you did. Whether or not you knew it, every time he talked about you, it was as if his shirt buttons were close to bursting. And when the chips were down, you came back to him."

"But I wasn't always there. Not like you." Chet paused, then said, "He thought of you like a son, Ty."

"Yes."

When Chet raised his face even more, there was a glint of pain in his shaded eyes. "I hated you for that sometimes."

Tyler could only nod.

But then Zoe's confident voice came to him. *You're a fixer...*

Chet's raw voice interrupted. "Even then, I could never hate you for long. You're not the kind of person who's easy to dislike."

That big-brotherly rush got to Tyler again, but before he could decide how to respond, Chet stood, as if to leave the room.

A fixer.

And even though Zoe wasn't here, Tyler felt her presence more strongly than ever.

He wanted to live up to what she thought of him.

"Where are you off to?" Tyler asked.

Chet shrugged, hands in his coat pockets. "I'm not really sure where I'm going."

"I have a good idea where you should be."

Hope lit up Chet's eyes, and it was too much for even Tyler.

He roughly wrapped an arm around his brother, and at first, Chet seemed stunned.

But then he hugged Tyler right back, holding him as if he didn't have much else.

Brother to brother.

Soon enough, they awkwardly patted each other on the backs, separating.

As Tyler handed the Polaroid back to Chet, he knew that there were other amends to be made, primarily with someone he needed more than ever. Someone he'd fallen for so hard that it had taken him a while to get back up, and if he lost her because of his stubbornness or because he was too much of a coward to take a chance, he didn't see how he could live with himself.

And that someone was back on Florence Ranch, probably packing up to leave.

"How about I drive you home now?" Tyler asked Chet.

It was the first time in the past few weeks he'd seen his youngest brother really smile.

Zoe had considered departing from the guesthouse tonight about a hundred times, but some cockeyed hope had kept her here, looking under the bed once more to see if she was leaving something behind, peering into the bathroom medicine cabinet, feeling as if there was something she hadn't packed.

It didn't take a genius to figure out what it was.

Tyler—and what if he changed his mind about her and she left before he got here?

She kept asking herself this question as she got ready for bed, putting on her cotton nightie and slathering lotion over her skin. But with each hour that crept by, she realized that he wasn't coming.

No matter how much she wanted him to.

She went to bed with half her face buried in the pillow, still not believing that he didn't care. Still feeling how he'd worshipped her body, how he'd seemed on the edge of saying something significant to her just before pulling back so many times.

But she wasn't going to cry.

Not her.

Not the woman who'd gotten what she'd come back

to Florence Ranch to get—respect. A sense of worth. A better relationship with her dad.

She must've floated off to sleep, because the next thing she knew, she heard his voice, woven into a dream.

"Zoe?"

She turned over, groggy, but still listening.

All she heard now were the crickets through the open window, the hovering sound of summer air…

But her heartbeat was the loudest of all, especially when she heard his voice again.

"Zoe!"

Firmer this time, even though the voice seemed to be at a distance.

A dream. This *had* to be a dream…

Not really convinced, she sat up in bed, peeking through the screen, where the flowers lined the window box.

And there he was, under the moonlight, the cowboy of her dreams.

Her veins tangled like a network of wires that sparked, but the zapping died when she thought of the last time she'd seen him, in his office, where he'd let her go.

"You're here?" she asked through the window. She'd promised Tyler she would be around for him, but hour after hour, she'd lost faith and the doubts had done their damage.

He moved toward her, and the buzz and sizzle of those sparks came back, burning her.

"You didn't leave," he said.

"First thing tomorrow."

"Then can I come in?"

To where? she wanted to ask. Come in to her heart? Because she'd already allowed him there, where no one else had ever been. And he'd tossed it aside, leaving behind a mess that she would eventually clean up, given time.

"If I let you in," she said, "would you stay?"

"Yes. God, yes. I was an idiot, Zoe. Seeing you again made me realize…"

And there he went, cutting himself off, leaving her stranded.

She wasn't sure she could take much more of this.

"When you're a bit surer," she said, sinking back down to her mattress and lying on her back, "let me know."

"Listen to me, Zoe."

He'd come to her window, but she stayed put on the bed. It was hard enough just hearing him, because his voice had a way of seeping in to her, conquering her from the inside out.

He took on a new tone.

"All my life, I've had everything. Some of it's been given to me, some of it was well-earned. Some of it's been taken away, and I got so used to that last part that I started to prepare myself for the inevitability every time I got too comfortable. And that's what you made me, Zoe—more comfortable than I could ever have imagined."

He was like a force of nature, continuing on, unstoppable.

"You gave me clarity, direction…" She could hear him leaning against the building. "You gave me love, Zoe, and I had no idea what to do with it."

Zoe couldn't move.

It felt as if her pulse was quivering. "Are you saying you love me?"

There was a smile in his voice. "I am. I love you. I love you so much that I can't stay away. And, in spite of all my faults, I'm a man of my word once I say it."

Tears began to pool in her eyes, blurring the room around her. Happy tears. Anxious tears.

Excited tears.

"Because of you," he said, "I even made my peace with Chet today. I brought him back here, to the big house."

"You did?"

Because of her.

"And I'm getting around to my dad. It took an angel to inspire me to do it."

An angel? *His* angel?

"You," he said. "Only and always you, Zoe."

Her pulse was a pounding summons.

So Zoe put her life in his, rolling out of bed, going to the door and opening it.

He was still by the window, leaning against the boards of the cottage. When he heard her, he pushed away from the wall, watching her as if she really was an angel in her short white summer nightgown.

Slowly, he walked toward her, and she wished he would get here a little faster.

One step.

Two…

Then he took one more long stride, rushing her, sweeping her into his arms and holding her up.

Her breath gushed out of her and she couldn't take in another one.

A view from the top, Zoe thought. This was it.

With painful deliberation, he let her slide down, her belly to his mouth, then her stomach. She wrapped her legs around him as they came face-to-face.

"Come inside," she said.

He mounted the steps and kicked the door shut behind them.

They stood there like that, looking at each other, and somewhere along the line they started walking, moving, knowing exactly where they were going.

When they got to the bedroom, he didn't presume anything. He only sat her down on the sheet-twisted mattress, her legs hanging over the side.

"I can't believe I'm here," he said. "I say that only because it took me so damn long."

"And how long can you stay now?"

"As long as you'll have me."

"Tyler..." she said, and the consent was in her voice.

With sensuous wonder, he clasped both his hands around her ankles, then slipped them up, caressing her calves, gliding his fingers behind her knees.

She jumped a little.

"Ticklish," he said, as if discovering this about her pleased him, and he would take even greater delight in finding out more.

Much more.

Her blood ran hot, spearing down to her belly. Then lower, where it came to a throbbing point between her legs.

As he continued his journey upward, his hands over her knees now, over her thighs, under her nightie, she leaned her head back, anticipating.

He eased off her panties, down, down, the lace

whispering against her skin. When he finished, tossing the material away, he parted her knees slightly, and the air trickled over her most private area.

From the way her chest was rising and falling, from the way she'd lowered her gaze at him, he obviously saw that she liked this, and he suspended the sultry moment, pausing as he disrobed.

When he came back to her, he had only his jeans on. It was more than enough to tickle her fancy, with his strong chest, those muscles in the moonlight that was coming from the window.

"My Zoe," he said, and the sexy endearment struck her hard, making her pound even more as he delved his hands under her nightie again, separating her legs wider.

He bent his head, and her heartbeat jerked, knowing what was coming next.

She wanted to lean her head back again, but she wanted to watch him, too. She couldn't tear her eyes away as he kissed a path from the inside of her knee to her inner thigh, then even farther...

Groaning, she fell to the mattress at the same time he got to the center of her, kissing her there thoroughly, lovingly.

She rested her hands on the back of his head as he stoked her up inside, a growing bonfire that melted her bones so that she didn't know how she was going to come out of this—in what shape. In what new form.

All she knew was that she was arching, rocking with every motion of his tongue and lips as she held back the pressure building in her core.

Gathering...

Flaring...swirling up and up until she—

Zoe let out a high cry that seemed to last forever until he slid up her body, catching the sounds of her with his mouth, taking her in, body and soul.

They kissed as if they'd never done it before, as if each time was the first—a new discovery, a new place where nothing else could touch them. She didn't even know when her nightie came off, but at some point, she was completely naked, as vulnerable as anyone could be until he covered her with his own bare length.

She could feel every muscle against her, from his thighs to his belly and chest. Her breasts were crushed under him, his erection nestled between her lower thighs until he moved up, brushing his tip through her folds.

Moaning, she wiggled underneath him.

Come in, she thought.

But he was teasing her, nipping at her mouth with his while nudging between her legs.

She was going to die if he didn't...

With a smooth thrust, he entered her, and she strained against him, lifting her hips, urging him on.

He moved in and out as the sweat on their bodies made their skin slippery, as she lost even more shape and form inside, becoming who she'd always wanted to be.

A woman who'd found the man she was going to spend the rest of her life with.

Waves seemed to roll from her toes to her head, pressing into her, down on her, kneading her while he kept driving and she kept panting, encouraging him, knowing he was getting closer—

Closer...

He stiffened, spilling inside her, burying his face in her neck until he shuddered. His climax pushed her forward, too, as her center seemed to rotate, stretch and pull, tearing her apart.

Pulling.

Spread every which way.

Stretching…

She snapped, her body slamming into itself, and she bit Tyler's shoulder at the ferocity of her pleasure while she came down.

Down.

As he held her, something gathered inside, shaping Zoe into her final form.

His woman, forever and always.

And she would bet it had formed a counterpart inside him as he kissed her again, two people made only for each other.

Epilogue

One Month Later

The night Tyler's world completely came together, he was sitting on a saddle above a small crowd seated in chairs on the lawn of Florence Ranch.

Right in front of the altar, his best men waited in their tuxedos, Stetsons and polished boots. But at the sight of Tyler mounted on a horse, Jeremiah whooped, then took off his hat and circled it in the air.

The crowd applauded in surprised delight, too. Even Chet, Tyler's second best man, cracked a smile, though it had been hard to get too many of those out of him since Abe's funeral.

Tyler urged Chance to the altar, then gave his horse a hearty few pats before dismounting. Keith, the foreman, took the reins and led the animal away, but even though the horse came to stand at a distance, Tyler imagined that Chance almost looked like a third best man.

Yet there were really only two—just as there were now merely two presidents of The Barron Group since Tyler had submitted his resignation.

He stood where the groom was supposed to stand, his heartbeat a wonderful tangle of rhythm. But he wasn't afraid of taking the vows that were coming his way.

He was a man of his word, and he would mean every one that he was about to say.

In the front row, his dad slumped in a chair, his bolo askew. Drunk again.

Tyler wasn't about to let that ruin this day as the "Wedding March" struck its first harp-and-violin chords.

When Zoe appeared in her long, white dress with a veil that draped over her shoulders, there was nothing else. Not even Miguel, who was escorting her.

There was just her, holding a rainbow of flowers, locking gazes with him, smiling under her veil.

His beautiful soul mate.

The ceremony flew by, until it was time to kiss the bride.

Tyler pushed back Zoe's veil, revealing those amazing blue-gray eyes.

He kissed her, soft, sweet.

The first kiss of the rest of their lives.

As more music sounded, he took Zoe's hand, and she laughed as he ran with her far over to where Chance stood on the lawn with Keith.

"What about bringing me back down the aisle?" she asked as he lifted her up to Chance's back.

Tyler mounted, too, pulling her over his lap.

"We're taking the long way around."

"But the guests and the photographer...?"

"The shutterbug can wait. As for the guests, they have the entire reception to see you. I want you to myself for a minute since we haven't been together since last night."

At the mention of their prewedding encounter, Zoe got that glowy look.

He urged Chance to a walk, then faster as the crowd cheered them on. But when they got far enough away, he slowed down his horse, kissing Zoe some more.

Kissing her until she sighed under his lips.

In the background, the band started up. The guests would be going into the ballroom now for food and fun.

"We've still got tonight, cowboy," she said.

She grinned, and he knew that she was going to make him wait.

It would be worth it, though.

He brought Chance around to where Keith was standing near the gardens, then took his Stetson from the foreman and put the hat on his head.

"Thanks, buddy," Tyler said to him.

Keith nodded. He was going to hand Chance off to one of the employees Tyler and Zoe had already hired for the horse rescue they were putting together. She'd retired from Walker & Associates, just as he'd done with The Group. They had even bought a ranch just a few miles away, on the fringes of Duarte Hill.

The photographer found the couple, then got his fill of them and the wedding party. By the time Zoe and Tyler peered just inside the big windows of the ballroom, things were in full swing.

In the corner, Tyler saw Jeremiah in the middle of a bunch of women.

"Jer's having a great time," Zoe said.

"An overly great one, as usual."

Like Tyler, Jeremiah was trying to find something to hold on to. A woman to make him feel truly alive.

Unlike Tyler, Jeremiah hadn't found that certain someone yet.

He saw his other brother in a far corner with his assistant, Mina Ferguson. They had a space between them, but Tyler noticed that she kept watching him, as if she wanted to comfort Chet, pull him out of the funk he'd fallen into this past month.

The music stopped, and Jeremiah bounded up to the stage, a glass of champagne in hand.

"Time to welcome our bride and groom!" he said.

Tyler held Zoe's hand. "That's our cue."

She stood on her tiptoes, kissing him just before the band struck up a tune, ushering them in. As the song segued into a slow country ballad, Tyler held his bride close.

Zoe, right at home in her fancy dress, dancing in the ballroom, just as they had that one night when he'd been too much of a fool to snatch her up right away.

He stroked her cheek, and she looked into his eyes, where he saw a reflection of himself. Of how much she loved him and he loved her.

They had the ballroom now, but tonight, they'd be staying in his cabin, nearer the pastures, the swimming hole.

They'd be a cowboy and his cowgirl.

Her mouth shaped the words *I love you,* but he wanted to say it out loud.

Wanted everyone to know.

"I love you, Zoe Barron," he said loudly, sweeping her off her feet as she laughed and everyone clapped.

Although she came back down to him, he felt as if they would both be flying high from this day forward.

* * * * *

Don't miss Jeremiah Barron's story,
Taming the Texas Playboy.
Coming soon to Silhouette Special Edition.

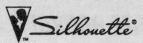

COMING NEXT MONTH

Available January 25, 2011

REQUEST YOUR FREE BOOKS!
2 FREE NOVELS PLUS 2 FREE GIFTS!

SPECIAL EDITION
Life, Love and Family!

YES! Please send me 2 FREE Silhouette® Special Edition® novels and my 2 FREE gifts (gifts are worth about $10). After receiving them, if I don't wish to receive any more books, I can return the shipping statement marked "cancel." If I don't cancel, I will receive 6 brand-new novels every month and be billed just $4.24 per book in the U.S. or $4.99 per book in Canada. That's a saving of 15% off the cover price! It's quite a bargain! Shipping and handling is just 50¢ per book.* I understand that accepting the 2 free books and gifts places me under no obligation to buy anything. I can always return a shipment and cancel at any time. Even if I never buy another book from Silhouette, the two free books and gifts are mine to keep forever.

235/335 SDN E5RG

Name	(PLEASE PRINT)	
Address		Apt. #
City	State/Prov.	Zip/Postal Code

Signature (if under 18, a parent or guardian must sign)

Mail to the Silhouette Reader Service:
IN U.S.A.: P.O. Box 1867, Buffalo, NY 14240-1867
IN CANADA: P.O. Box 609, Fort Erie, Ontario L2A 5X3

Not valid for current subscribers to Silhouette Special Edition books.

Want to try two free books from another line?
Call 1-800-873-8635 or visit www.morefreebooks.com.

* Terms and prices subject to change without notice. Prices do not include applicable taxes. N.Y. residents add applicable sales tax. Canadian residents will be charged applicable provincial taxes and GST. Offer not valid in Quebec. This offer is limited to one order per household. All orders subject to approval. Credit or debit balances in a customer's account(s) may be offset by any other outstanding balance owed by or to the customer. Please allow 4 to 6 weeks for delivery. Offer available while quantities last.

Your Privacy: Silhouette is committed to protecting your privacy. Our Privacy Policy is available online at www.eHarlequin.com or upon request from the Reader Service. From time to time we make our lists of customers available to reputable third parties who may have a product or service of interest to you. If you would prefer we not share your name and address, please check here. ☐

Help us get it right—We strive for accurate, respectful and relevant communications. To clarify or modify your communication preferences, visit us at www.ReaderService.com/consumerschoice.

SSE10R

HARLEQUIN®

A *Romance*

FOR EVERY MOOD™

Spotlight on
Classic

Quintessential, modern love stories
that are romance at its finest.

See the next page
to enjoy a sneak peek from
the Harlequin® Romance series.

*Harlequin Romance author Donna Alward is loved
for her gorgeous rancher heroes.*

*Meet Wyatt as he's confronted by both a precious
little pink bundle left on his doorstep and his neighbor Elli
who's going to show him the ropes....*

Introducing
PROUD RANCHER, PRECIOUS BUNDLE

THE SQUAWKING QUIETED as Elli picked the baby up, and
Wyatt turned around, trying hard to ignore the feelings of
inadequacy as Darcy immediately stopped fussing.

"Maybe she's uncomfortable. What do you think, sweetheart?" Elli turned her conversation to the baby.

"What do you think is wrong?" Wyatt asked, putting the
coffee pot back on the burner.

A strange look passed over Elli's face, one that looked
like guilt and panic. But it was gone quickly. "I couldn't
say," she replied.

"But you were so good with her this afternoon." Wyatt
put his hands on his hips.

"Lucky, that's all. I just...remembered a few things."
The same strange look flitted over her features once more.

Wyatt took the coffee to the table. "You fooled me. You
looked like you knew exactly what you were doing." So
much so that Wyatt had felt completely inept. A feeling he
despised. He was used to being the one in control.

Elli and Darcy walked the length of the kitchen and
back. After a few moments, she admitted, "I haven't really
cared for a baby before. The things I thought of were simply
things I'd heard about. Not from experience, Mr. Black."

Her chin jutted up, closing the subject but making him

want to ask the questions now pulsing through his mind. But then he remembered the old saying—*Don't look a gift horse in the mouth.* He'd benefit from whatever insight she had and be glad of it.

"I don't really know what babies need," he said. "I fed her, patted her back like you did, walked her to sleep, but every time I put her down…"

Wyatt almost groaned. Of course. He'd forgotten one important thing. He'd been so focused on getting the formula the right temperature that he'd forgotten to check her diaper. Not that he had any clue what to do there either.

Pulling calves and shoveling out stalls was far less intimidating than one tiny newborn.

"She's probably due for a diaper change, isn't she." He tried to sound nonchalant. This was a perfect opportunity. Elli must know how to change a diaper. He could simply watch her so he'd know better for the next time.

Instead, Elli came around the corner of the counter and placed Darcy back in his arms. "Here you go, Uncle Wyatt," she said lightly. "You get diaper duty. I'll fix the coffee. Cream and sugar?"

Oh boy, Wyatt thought, looking down into Darcy's pursed face, his smug plan blown to smithereens. He was in for it now.

Will sparks fly between Elli and Wyatt?

Find out in
PROUD RANCHER, PRECIOUS BUNDLE

Available February 2011 from Harlequin Romance

Try these Healthy and Delicious Spring Rolls!

INGREDIENTS

2 packages rice-paper spring roll wrappers (20 wrappers)

1 cup grated carrot

¼ cup bean sprouts

1 cucumber, julienned

1 red bell pepper, without stem and seeds, julienned

4 green onions finely chopped—use only the green part

DIRECTIONS

1. Soak one rice-paper wrapper in a large bowl of hot water until softened.

2. Place a pinch each of carrots, sprouts, cucumber, bell pepper and green onion on the wrapper toward the bottom third of the rice paper.

3. Fold ends in and roll tightly to enclose filling.

4. Repeat with remaining wrappers. Chill before serving.

Find this and many more delectable recipes including the perfect dipping sauce in

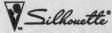

Silhouette®

ROMANTIC
S U S P E N S E

Sparked by Danger, Fueled by Passion.

NEW YORK TIMES BESTSELLING AUTHOR
RACHEL LEE

No Ordinary Hero

Strange noises...a woman's mysterious disappearance
and a killer on the loose who's too close for comfort.

With no where else to turn, Delia Carmody looks
to her aloof neighbour to help, only to discover
that Mike Windwalker is no ordinary hero.

Conard
County *THE NEXT GENERATION*

Available in February.
Wherever books are sold.

HARLEQUIN *Presents*

USA TODAY bestselling author

Sharon Kendrick

introduces

HIS MAJESTY'S CHILD

The king's baby of shame!

King Casimiro harbors a secret—no one in the kingdom of Zaffirinthos knows that a devastating accident has left his memory clouded in darkness. And Casimiro himself cannot answer why Melissa Maguire, an enigmatic English rose, stirs such feelings in him…,. Questioning his ability to rule, Casimiro decides he will renounce the throne. But Melissa has news she knows will rock the palace to its core—*Casimiro has an heir!*

Law dictates Casimiro cannot abdicate, so he must find a way to reacquaint himself with Melissa—his new queen!

Available from Harlequin Presents
February 2011

www.eHarlequin.com

HP12972